KNIGHTS TO THE RESCUE!

"Kellach! Driskoll! Are you in there? I need your help!"

"Moyra!" Kellach raced across the room to the large wooden door, with Driskoll not far behind. As Kellach wrenched the door open, Driskoll could see their friend over his brother's shoulder. Her red hair was dripping and plastered against her head, her eyes sparked with panic, and her blue jacket was totally soaked.

She didn't seem to care.

"You boys have to help me!" she gasped. "It's my mother! She's been arrested!"

Kellach and Driskoll blinked.

"Didn't you hear me? They've taken her to Watchers' Hall. And they say they might hang her!"

THE HIDDEN DRAGON

LISA TRUTKOFF TRUMBAUER

BOOK 7

COVER & INTERIOR ART
EMILY FIEGENSCHUH

MIRROR
STONE

The Hidden Dragon

©2005 Wizards of the Coast, Inc.

Cover and interior art by Emily Fiegenschuh
Cartography by Dennis Kauth
First Printing: June 2005
Library of Congress Catalog Card Number: 2004116902

9 8 7 6 5 4 3 2 1

US ISBN: 0-7869-3748-3
ISBN-13: 978-0-7869-3748-6
620-96702000-001-EN

U.S., CANADA,
ASIA, PACIFIC, & LATIN AMERICA
Wizards of the Coast, Inc.
P.O. Box 707
Renton, WA 98057-0707
+1-800-324-6496

EUROPEAN HEADQUARTERS
Hasbro UK Ltd
Caswell Way
Newport, Gwent NP9 0YH
GREAT BRITAIN
Please keep this address for your records

Visit our web site at **www.mirrorstonebooks.com**

For my mother-in-law, Bonnie B. Trumbauer

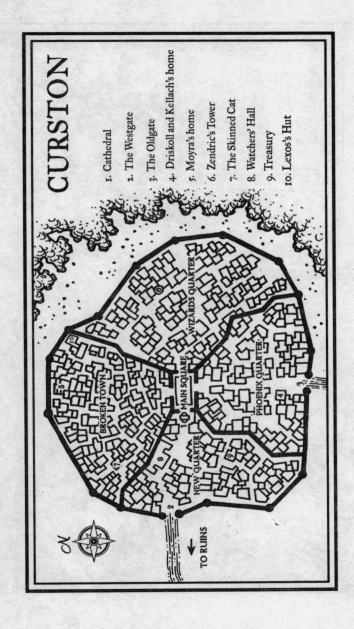

CURSTON

1. Cathedral
2. The Westgate
3. The Oldgate
4. Driskoll and Kellach's home
5. Moyra's home
6. Zendric's Tower
7. The Skinned Cat
8. Watchers' Hall
9. Treasury
10. Lexos's Hut

BROKEN TOWN

WIZARDS QUARTER

MAIN SQUARE

NEW QUARTER

PHOENIX QUARTER

TO RUINS

CHAPTER

1

The young warrior waved his sword high above his head. The cyclops charged, its single eye gleaming. The warrior waited for the right moment . . . steady . . . steady. . . . Now! With one quick thrash, he brought his sword down and—

"Driskoll!" Kellach yelled. "Will you watch what you're doing? You nearly brought that thing down on my head."

Driskoll slowly refocused. The fierce cyclops he saw in his mind disappeared to be replaced by his brother.

Driskoll wasn't sure which one looked more annoyed—the cyclops or Kellach.

Driskoll hastily drew back his sword. "Sorry, Kell, but geez—you get to train for being a great wizard some day. How am I ever supposed to train for being a great warrior?"

"For starters, lad, you can train outdoors," said Zendric.

"But it's raining," Driskoll pointed out, plàcing the sword back in the scabbard attached to his belt.

"All the more reason why you should leave your sword sheathed," the wizard continued. "After all, you don't want it getting tarnished, now, do you?"

"Get tarnished? Inside?" Driskoll scoffed.

Driskoll could see, however, that his words fell on deaf ears. Kellach and Zendric had already gone back to their lesson. Kellach was training to be a powerful wizard, like Zendric. Although Kellach and Driskoll were both members of the old order, the order known as the Knights of the Silver Dragon, Kellach was the one who had the talent to be a wizard. And Zendric was the only wizard left in Curston who still followed the old ways. He hoped to pass his magical knowledge on to Kellach.

Which often left Driskoll at odds with what to do with himself.

Especially when it rained.

Zendric and Kellach stood before a long, wooden worktable, which took up most of the central floor space of the tower room. On the table, Driskoll saw a large book of spells. As Driskoll watched, Zendric raised his arms dramatically. Kellach did the same, following his teacher's example.

Beyond the table, on the far side of the room, was a large fireplace—so large, in fact, that Driskoll could nearly stand straight up inside it. A fire glowed there now, warming the room.

Driskoll strolled around the tower room, the musty smell of books and dust heightened by the chilly rain from outdoors. His boots slapped softly along the stone floor.

"Driskoll, what is your problem today?" Kellach asked, stopping in mid-chant. "I can't concentrate with you banging around here like this."

"Sorry, Kell," Driskoll said for the second time in as many

minutes. He plopped himself down between two large piles of books and leaned back against the wall. As quietly as possible, he drew his sword, once again imagining thwarting invisible beasts and saving his hometown of Curston. In his mind, he set his battle to music, knowing one day he'd not only be a great warrior, but a great bard as well, recounting his tales of bravery in song and prose.

Unfortunately, the stacks of books he lightly stabbed were not as stable as they had appeared. Driskoll watched, dumbstruck, as the stacks wobbled, then toppled over with a huge crash.

"Driskoll!"

This time, both Zendric and Kellach shouted his name.

Although Zendric and Kellach might have been about sixty years apart in age, their faces had the same scowl.

Driskoll hung his head. "Sorry—" he began. Then something caught his eye.

"Hey, Kell! Look at this!" Driskoll picked up one of the books that had tumbled from the stack. It had fallen with its pages open, staring up at him. The image on the page caught his eye. Monsters!

"If it's not a book of spells, I'm not interested," Kellach said.

"*A Practical Guide to Monsters*," Driskoll read as he closed the book to see the title. "Written by—"

"Driskoll!" Zendric threw up his hands. "You are completely wasting our practice time."

"But this book—Zendric, you wrote it!"

Zendric sighed and lowered his arms.

Kellach's eyes widened. "Zendric, is that true?"

3

"Indeed, lads, I penned that tome, quite some time ago." Zendric walked slowly to the chair beside the fireplace and lowered himself into it. "I had thought that by describing—no, by explaining the monsters that lived among us—that people would have a better understanding of them."

Kellach walked over to his brother and sat beside him on the floor. He peered at the book in Driskoll's lap. "What are you saying, Zendric? That monsters once lived freely among the people of Curston?"

Zendric nodded. "They did, many, many years ago, before the monsters were trapped behind the seal."

"You mean the seal that broke five years ago and released the monsters again?" Kellach asked.

"That's right. Long before you lads were born, some monsters lived quite happily among the people of Curston. Then slowly, the monsters began to turn on us, and the ruling council decided we had no choice but to banish all the evil monsters to the place behind the seal. When that seal was broken, all the rage the monsters had felt from their confinement was unleashed."

"And that's when the Knights of the Silver Dragon fell," Kellach said.

"That's right, Kellach. The Knights fought valiantly, but it wasn't enough. I'm still not sure why I survived, but I must have been left here to usher in a new order of the Knights."

Kellach and Driskoll looked at each other and smiled. Along with their friend Moyra, the brothers had been inducted into the order after committing a stunning act of bravery. Now they worked to help Zendric restore the Knights and bring peace back to their town of Curston.

"Hey, look at this," Driskoll said, pausing on one page in the book.

Kellach glanced over his shoulder. "It looks like a silver dragon—a *real* silver dragon." Kellach looked up at Zendric. "Is that possible?"

"Of course," Zendric said with a wave of his hand. "The order of knights was named after a most royal of beasts."

"So a silver dragon was a monster?" Driskoll asked.

"Not so much in the way that you mean, lad," Zendric said. "Silver dragons were wild creatures that once roamed freely in the mountains. They were known throughout the region as solitary, gentle beings."

"So not all monsters are evil, then?" Kellach asked.

"On the contrary. Only those monsters kept behind the seal were evil, for they wanted to battle each other—and us—for supremacy."

Driskoll shivered. "That's what we sometimes hear beyond the walls of Curston, isn't it? The sounds of the monsters fighting each other?"

Zendric nodded. "That's right. Now the safest place for us remains here in Curston, although, as you know, we often have our own problems."

As if on cue, a loud banging disrupted their conversation, accompanied by a girl's frantic shouts.

"Kellach! Driskoll! Are you in there? I need your help!"

"Moyra!" Kellach raced across the room to the large wooden door, with Driskoll not far behind. As Kellach wrenched the door open, Driskoll could see their friend over his brother's shoulder. Her red hair was dripping and plastered against her head, her eyes sparked with panic, and her blue jacket was totally soaked.

She didn't seem to care.

"You boys have to help me!" she gasped. "It's my mother! She's been arrested!"

Kellach and Driskoll blinked.

"Didn't you hear me? They've taken her to Watchers' Hall. And they say they might hang her!"

CHAPTER

2

Slow down!" Kellach said, grabbing Moyra's arm and pulling her inside. He closed the door behind her. "What are you talking about?"

"Your mother would never break the law," Driskoll said.

"I know!" Moyra panted, trying to catch her breath. "That's why this is so insane. And that's why we don't have time to talk. We have to leave—now!"

Kellach glanced over at Zendric.

"Be off with you," Zendric said with a wave, staring down at the mess of books scattered haphazardly across the floor. "As it is, I must clean up after Driskoll and the tomes he enjoyed battling."

"I didn't do it on purpose," Driskoll muttered.

"We don't have time for this!" Moyra yelled, as she threw open the door. "Let's go!"

Kellach and Driskoll dashed out after Moyra. But at the last moment, Driskoll remembered to shut the door. As Driskoll turned back toward the tower, he caught a glimpse of the old wizard through the doorframe. As Zendric picked up one of the fallen books, a look of astonishment creeped across his face.

Closing the book slowly, Zendric said to no one, "So. The time has come."

"You know, I wouldn't even need your help, if it wasn't for your stupid father," Moyra said as they jogged through the wet streets of Curston, dodging fruit carts, townspeople dashing for cover, and the occasional scrawny stray cat.

Kellach and Driskoll glanced at each other and smiled knowingly. Moyra tried to be tough, but they both knew she wasn't as hard as she appeared.

"It's okay, Moyra," Kellach said. "We'll see what's going on."

"What did your mom do, anyway?" Driskoll asked.

"Your dad claims she was accused of stealing some sort of medallion." She scoffed.

"A medallion?" Kellach repeated. "Who would accuse your mom of stealing a medallion?"

"That's what makes the whole thing so weird." Moyra paused to catch her breath, stopped at the edge of Curston's Main Square. "When I asked Torin who had accused my mom of stealing the medallion, he shut up like one of the dungeons at the bottom of the prison. I couldn't pry any information from him. That's when I knew Mom was in serious trouble."

Kellach nodded sagely. "Dad will tell us. I'm sure of it."

The trio sprinted across Main Square and down another cobblestone street. Soon they stood before the walls of Watchers' Hall, below which lay Curston's prison.

8

The Hall stretched from one end of the block to the other. The fact that the town prison lay directly beneath Watchers' Hall did nothing to help the building's reputation. Sprawled along the edge of Broken Town—the roughest neighborhood of Curston—it stood as a reminder of the authority of the watch.

Kellach, Driskoll, and Moyra burst through the doors of Watchers' Hall. They raced through the base of the tower and tore past the spiral staircase that led upward into the tower. Finally they reached the foyer, where they stumbled up to the duty desk.

"My father!" Kellach panted to the elderly man perched behind the desk. "Where is he?"

Guffy appeared startled, but not surprised to see the boys. He leaned on a tall stool, balancing his weight on one single leg. The other leg he'd lost to a werewolf during the battles that followed the Sundering of the Seal. The stone counter had a wooden top, and Guffy had the day's newssheets spread across it.

"And a good day to you, too, boy!" said Guffy warmly. He'd known the boys since they could first walk. In fact, with the captain of the watch as their father, Driskoll and Kellach had practically grown up at Watchers' Hall. "In a bit of a hurry today, are you?"

"We have serious business to talk to my father about," Driskoll said.

"When do you not?" Guffy chuckled. "You'll find him in his office. I think you know—"

They didn't wait for Guffy to finish. Kellach, Driskoll, and Moyra hurried down the hallway until they reached the stone arch that led to Torin's office. When they entered, Torin was seated behind his desk, issuing orders to two watchers. Kellach, Driskoll, and Moyra waited impatiently for Torin to finish his business. It probably took only half a minute, but it seemed to Driskoll that an eternity had crept by.

Finally, the two watchers marched past them and out the archway. Before Kellach could even utter a word, his father began shaking his head.

"I know why you're here, son, and I can't help you."

Kellach strode forward and stood respectfully before his father's desk, just as the two watchers had done. "Dad, Moyra's mother is innocent."

"That's not what we've been told." Torin sighed.

Moyra rushed forward. "My mom didn't steal some stupid medallion!"

Torin looked kindly at the girl, but his jaw and his resolve remained firm. "The situation is out of my hands."

"Dad, you're the captain of the watch!" Driskoll said. "Nothing is ever out of your hands."

"Son, I just maintain the laws. I don't make them. And, according to my sources, Moyra's mother has broken the law. And now she must pay the consequences." Torin rustled through some sheets of parchment on his desk, until he found the one he was looking for. He held it out to Moyra. "See? It says right here on your mother's arrest report."

Driskoll watched the red drop from Moyra's cheeks. "Arrest report?"

"Yes," Torin said crisply. "It states here that Royma was in possession of a medallion that had been reported stolen."

"Who reported it stolen?" Kellach demanded.

"Don't use that tone with me, son. You know how these things work. I cannot tell you that information. It's confidential."

Kellach opened his mouth to say more, when Driskoll cut him off. "What else does the report say?"

"It says here," Torin continued, "that Royma was arrested in her stall at the marketplace, at the break of dawn."

Moyra nodded her head. "This time of year, Mom always gets there early to sell the herbs she grows in her garden."

"Yes, well, two watchers approached her as she was setting up, and they asked her to empty her pockets. The medallion was found in the pocket of her cloak."

"Wait a minute," Kellach interrupted. "You mean, no one actually saw Royma steal the medallion?"

Torin stared uncertainly at the report. "Er, um, no."

"Well, then, how did they know Royma had the medallion to begin with?" Driskoll asked.

"Because the medallion was stolen, and someone suspected her of the crime."

"And that leads us back to the big question," Moyra said.

All three children looked pointedly at the captain of the watch.

"Who?" they said together.

Torin sat back and sighed. He steepled his fingers before his lips and contemplated the trio before him. Driskoll, Kellach, and Moyra waited breathlessly for his answer.

"I didn't want to tell you this because I knew you would get all worked up about it."

"Tell us what?" Kellach asked earnestly.

"It's Lexos. He's been released."

Moyra gasped.

Driskoll's jaw dropped.

Only Kellach seemed able to form any words. "You—you let Lexos out of prison? That lunatic? That crazy, demented, dangerous, power-hungry egomaniac?"

Kellach took a deep breath. "Dad, have you completely lost your mind?"

CHAPTER

3

Torin slowly rose from his chair and glared at his oldest son. Driskoll didn't think he'd ever seen his father that angry. Well, maybe a few times. But his anger now was just about as fierce as it ever got.

"You forget yourself, Kellach," Torin said evenly, resting the flats of his palms against the top of the desk. "First, you come into my office, disturb my work, and demand information, which I grudgingly convey to you." He paused for effect. When he spoke again, his voice was even more ominous. "Then you have the nerve to tell me, your father, that I have lost my mind? I think, my son, it is you who have lost *your* mind. And your manners. You will apologize immediately."

Kellach bowed his head.

"I'm sorry, Dad," Kellach began.

Torin nodded, and sank back into his wooden chair.

"But I still think that you've lost your mind!" Kellach looked his father in the eye. "How could you have released that madman back into Curston?"

Torin shook his head wearily. "Kellach, he's old. He's served enough time inside a dark, dirty cell."

"He's fooled you, Dad!" Driskoll joined in.

"Driskoll, are you calling your father a fool?"

"Well, no, but—"

"I've heard enough." Torin banged his fist against his desk like a judge's gavel. "Facts are facts. And the facts are that Royma had a medallion that Lexos said was stolen from him."

"And you believe his word over my mother's?" Moyra cried, placing her hands on her hips. "My mother's never done anything to anyone! And that evil man should rot in prison for all the harm he's done to this town."

Torin's face turned red and Driskoll could see that his father was about to yell at Moyra.

Driskoll jumped in. "Don't you remember how he almost killed Zendric?"

"*Almost* is the important word there, son. Think of it as Lexos having a lapse in judgment. Remember, he was, at one time, the town magistrate and the highest-ranking cleric at the Cathedral of St. Cuthbert. His service to Curston counts for something in the minds of the watch."

"And obviously in your mind too," Kellach said quietly. "So where is this medallion now?"

"At the moment it's in the treasury. And until this matter has been resolved, it must remain there."

"Really?" Driskoll said. "I bet old Lexos wasn't happy with that."

"As I said, he was the town magistrate. He knows the laws as well as anyone. He's changed, boys. You'll see."

Driskoll felt like a spider had just been dropped down his shirt. "What do you mean, we'll see?"

"Well, now that Lexos has been released, I'm sure you'll see him about town."

Driskoll studied his father for a moment, trying to see the joke in all this. But his father was totally serious. Driskoll caught Kellach's eye, and he could tell that his brother was just as shocked by their father's attitude as he was.

Something very odd was going on, and somehow it involved the elusive medallion.

"Sir," Moyra said as respectfully as possible. "Could I see my mother?"

"Yes, you probably should," said Torin. "After all, this case is moving along rather swiftly. Lexos still knows how to pull strings in this town, and he made sure that Royma was sentenced immediately after her arrest."

Moyra's cheeks flushed with anger again. "Sentenced? Was she even found guilty?"

"With Lexos's testimony, that wasn't a problem."

"But this is crazy!" Moyra shouted. "She's never committed a crime in her life! That has to mean something around here."

Torin gathered the papers on his desk. "I know this is hard to accept, but when someone commits a crime, punishment must follow. That's the way the law works. In this case, since the medallion is so valuable, Lexos requested the swiftest, harshest punishment."

"You mean . . . " Moyra croaked.

Torin looked up, nodding his head slowly. "The hanging has already been scheduled for the day after tomorrow. "

Driskoll saw the emotions race across Moyra's face—rage,

fear, sorrow. He gave Moyra credit for not losing it, right there in front of his dad.

"I can't believe you'd allow this to happen," she said in a deadly calm voice.

Torin shrugged. "It's not up to me. Now, I suggest you see your mother. I think we've talked about this all we can."

Driskoll watched as Moyra held her head high and marched from the room. Driskoll was sure he'd finally see Moyra collapse, but he should have known better. By the time he'd reached the hallway, Moyra was in a full-blown rage.

"This is totally ridiculous!" she seethed. "My mother did not steal some stupid medallion, especially from Lexos! Err! And your father! Why did he just sit there like that and defend Lexos? How could he?"

Kellach had a hard time finding an answer for that one. "I would think Dad would be just as outraged as we are."

"Instead, he had only nice things to say about Lexos," Driskoll said. "It doesn't make any sense."

"No, it doesn't," Kellach said. He turned to Moyra. "Come on, let's see your mom."

The trio walked quickly back through the corridors and into the foyer to find Guffy still engrossed in his reading. He greeted them without looking up. "Ah, children, back again, I see. What can I do for you now?"

"We've come to see my mother," Moyra said sharply, hands on her hips, daring the watcher to deny them access.

"Moyra, is it?" said looking up from the newssheets and eyeing Moyra suspiciously. "Your mother is Royma, the one that stole the magistrate's medallion?"

"First of all," Moyra began, "she didn't steal anything. And secondly, Lexos is not the magistrate!"

"Yes, yes, you're right, of course. I just remember the days when he was, and it's hard for me to think of him as anything but the town magistrate."

"There seems to be a lot of that going around," Driskoll said to Kellach.

"What's that, eh?"

"Um, nothing," Kellach said quickly. "Can we go in and see her, then?"

"Does your father know you're here?"

"Of course," Kellach said with authority.

Guffy hesitated for a moment, then he began to fumble with his keys. He turned to the thick, ironbound door behind his desk. Driskoll could hear Moyra tapping her foot as the watcher tried various keys before finally releasing all six locks. The locks had only been added recently, and Guffy obviously hadn't grown accustomed to them just yet.

At last, the door creaked open on its metal hinges, revealing a dark tunnel beyond.

"Don't be too long," Guffy warned. "I'll come get you in a few minutes. Royma's cell is on the first floor, fifth down on the right."

They headed into the tunnel and down the spiral stone staircase. Torches were placed unevenly along the wall, not giving much light to the small, narrow passage. Driskoll shivered as the cool, damp air of the prison brushed against the skin on his arms. He heard the trickle of water coming from somewhere below, and he thought he heard a moan drift up the stairway. "Probably the wind," he said to himself, trying to shake off the uneasy feeling he always had when he entered the prison.

Driskoll squared his shoulders and wrapped a fist around the hilt of his sword.

They reached the bottom of the stairway, and Moyra rushed ahead into the corridor beyond. Driskoll saw a few hands poke from the bars, but the depth of the darkness did not reveal any faces.

"Mom!" Moyra cried.

As Driskoll approached, he saw Royma sitting on a wooden bench against the wall, her dark red hair covering her face, her hands clenched in front of her.

When she heard Moyra's voice, she lifted her head and smiled thinly. Her eyes were the same green color as Moyra's, but they lacked the spark that lit Moyra's eyes from the inside.

"Bet you been wishing your whole life that you'd see your mean, old mother down here, haven't you?" She laughed, but the sound did not have much humor.

"Oh, Mom, don't talk like that! We know you didn't do this. We're working to get you out."

Royma stood and approached the bars. "Trouble is, girl, I might be guilty as charged."

"Of course you're not!" Moyra cried. "How can you say that?"

"Well, I did have that old medallion on my person, didn't I?"

"Where exactly did you find the medallion?" Kellach asked, stepping forward.

Royma placed her hand in her pocket, as if feeling the medallion there. "I was digging in my garden, like always, pulling up some fresh herbs to sell at the market, when what do you know? The bright, shiny thing fell into my hand."

"You mean, it was buried in the ground?" Driskoll asked.

Royma nodded. "It was quite beautiful. Unlike anything I'd ever set my eyes on. I could have stared at it all day, but I had to get my gardening done, didn't I? So I put the medallion in my pocket. I completely forgot about it until those idiot watchers came up to me." She scowled. "And I think you know what happened then."

"See?" Moyra flung over her shoulder at her friends. "I told you she didn't steal it."

"We never doubted that," Driskoll said. "But all the same, we need to figure out why Lexos is accusing her of having done so."

"Lexos?" Royma asked. "I thought he was dead."

Moyra's lip tightened. "Not yet, he isn't. But if I had my way, he would be," she muttered.

Kellach glanced at Moyra and cleared his throat. He leaned in closer to Royma. "Did you tell my father that you found the medallion in your yard?"

"I did at that," Royma said. "Your good-for-nothing father. He didn't believe me! He asked if I had found it, why didn't I wear it, like normal folk. He asked me why I was hiding it."

"And what did you say?" Kellach asked.

"I told the truth! That I had been in the garden and hadn't wanted to lose the pretty thing. So I had put it in my pocket. Just goes to show, the truth doesn't get you anywhere in this godsforsaken town." Royma kicked at the molding hay covering the cell floor.

Moyra reached her hand through the bars of the prison cell and laid it upon her mother's arm. "Don't worry, Mom. We're going to take care of it. We'll have this straightened out in no time."

The three were silent as they made their way back up through the prison, back through Watchers' Hall, and onto the street. The sky had cleared, and the sun shone brightly, creating sparkles that glinted off the wet cobblestones.

"What are we going to do now?" Driskoll asked, looking up at his older brother.

"Well, the way I see it," Kellach began, "we only have one choice."

"Which is?" Moyra asked.

"We must pay a visit to a madman."

CHAPTER

4

W hat are you talking about?" Driskoll said.

"It's obvious," Kellach continued. "Lexos is the one who has accused Moyra's mom. The only way to help Royma is to get him to drop the charges. Which means that we have to meet with him."

"Let's go." Moyra turned to run ahead.

"Wait a minute!" Driskoll said, grabbing her arm. "We don't even know where he is. And besides, we can't just march up to him and say, 'Hey, Lex old buddy, remember us? Good to see you again. And by the way—could you drop the charges against Moyra's mom?' I can hear his laugh now, and it's not a nice one."

"Driskoll has a point," Kellach said. "We need a plan."

"Maybe we need to figure out why that medallion is so important to Lexos in the first place," Driskoll said.

"Maybe what we need," Moyra said excitedly, "is the medallion itself!"

Kellach and Driskoll looked at her as if she'd grown an extra head.

"And how do you propose we do that?" Driskoll asked.

Moyra shrugged. "Steal it?"

"Are you cracked?" Driskoll asked. "How are we going to steal the medallion from the treasury? It's the most secure building in all of Curston. It's guarded around the clock by the watch."

Moyra sighed. "We'll just have to figure out some way. If we have the medallion, we can exchange it for my mom. I'm sure the medallion is more important to Lexos than my mom being in prison."

Kellach nodded. "She does have a point. The medallion will only be returned to its owner after the case is officially closed."

"That must be why Royma is getting executed so quickly." Driskoll felt sorry for saying the words as soon as they'd left his mouth, especially when he saw Moyra wince. "Sorry, Moyra. I didn't mean anything by that. I'm just trying to figure out this mess."

"Believe me, so am I," Moyra said as she began stomping down the street. When she realized that Kellach and Driskoll were not behind her, she turned abruptly. "Well, are you coming, or what?"

Moving to catch up, Driskoll asked, "Where are we going?"

"To find Breddo, of course," Moyra said. "If there's one thief in all of Curston who can tell us how to break into the treasury, it's him."

Driskoll stopped short. "Uh, don't get offended or anything, Moyra, but your dad does have a reputation for, well, you know."

"For what?" Moyra snapped.

Kellach cleared his throat and looked uncomfortable. "He's not exactly the best thief in all of Curston."

"And your point is?" Moyra said, clenching her fists.

Driskoll could practically feel the irritation flowing from her. He knew how sensitive she was about her father. Breddo was a good-natured man, but he had a tendency to steal, pick pockets, and conduct other sorts of petty crimes—and he was frequently caught in the act.

"All I mean is . . ." Kellach stuttered. "I mean maybe we shouldn't be getting advice about stealing the medallion from someone who spends so much time in prison."

Moyra's glare only became fiercer. "Do you have someone better in mind?"

Kellach paused for a moment but he had to admit defeat. He shook his head.

Moyra smirked. "Well, then, follow me."

❚ ❚ ❚ ❚ ❚

Driskoll gazed at the establishment in front of which they had stopped. A placard swung from a rusted chain above the door, bearing the name the Skinned Cat. Appropriately, a hairless panther had been painted on the wooden sign.

"Um, Moyra?" Driskoll asked. "Are you sure you want to go in here?

The Skinned Cat was one of Curston's many drinking holes, but this one was notorious for the odd mix of people who went there. *Odd* was a polite way to describe the Skinned Cat's customers.

"What?" Moyra looked over her shoulder at Driskoll. "The Skinned Cat is where my dad usually hangs out. You want to talk to my dad about getting into the treasury and stealing the medallion, don't you?"

Kellach ruffled Driskoll's hair. "Come on, Driskoll, you're not afraid, are you?"

"No . . ." Driskoll pushed Kellach's hand away.

Moyra shrugged. "I don't have time for this. I'll see you two inside." She pulled the rough-hewn door open, and with a quick smile, she disappeared.

"Right behind you!" Kellach called, and he slipped through the doorway, just before the door swung to a close.

"Wait—" Driskoll called. His stomach filled with butterflies. He rested his hand on the hilt of his sword. It was now or never. He pulled the door open and entered the Skinned Cat.

It was the odor that met Driskoll first, a mix of stale food, foul smoke, and—was that wet dog? Yep, the smell of wet dog. And something burning, maybe? Driskoll didn't want to even speculate what that something might be. Driskoll's ears became attuned to the rush of noise, a jostle of conversations, outbursts of laughter, and an occasional angry shout.

Great.

The main floor was dotted with tables. A long oak bar lined the entire right wall of the pub. Stools were pushed up to its edge. Dwarves and elves, gnomes and half-orcs shared space at the counter, either shoveling food into their mouths or hoisting tankards, steaming with brew.

He didn't see Moyra and Kellach anywhere. Where had they gone?

The last time they had come to the Skinned Cat, Moyra had led them through a maze of rooms at the back of the place. Not seeing Kellach and Moyra, Driskoll made his way toward the back. He wove across the tavern floor, dodging chairs and tables. He kept his hand on the hilt of his sword and his gaze trained for any trouble.

Finally he found the dark corridor he remembered from their last visit. He had hoped to see Kellach and Moyra about to enter one of the rooms, but no such luck. How had they gotten so far ahead of him? Driskoll wondered.

Slowly he began to walk down the dark passageway, peering into rooms to find his friends. From one room came a lot of shouting and cheering. Standing in the doorway, Driskoll saw a group of humans, dwarfs, and half-orcs gathered around a long box with legs, like a table with sides.

Stepping on his tiptoes, Driskoll peeked into the box. There he saw tiny winged impish creatures riding on the backs of rats. Lengths of yarn had been wound around the rats' jaws to keep them shut, and the imps held the ends of the yarn like one would hold the reins of a horse. The rats were racing one another down the length of the table, and the crowd of humans, dwarfs, and half-orcs cheered them on.

An old half-orc suddenly stepped in front of Driskoll. "Wanna place a bet, sonny?"

"Um, no. Sorry. I'm just looking for someone."

The half-orc's eyes narrowed. He leaned forward until his sharp tusks brushed Driskoll's cheek. His breath smelled like rotten meat. "This ain't no free show," the half-orc growled. "Place a bet. Or get out."

Driskoll ran out the door. He continued to roam down the hallway, glancing into rooms, shaking his head at the extreme weirdness of the things he saw. When he reached the last room and still hadn't found Kellach and Moyra, Driskoll began to stumble back up toward the main room of the tavern.

"I must have missed them somehow," he said out loud. Reaching the main area again, he stood in the opening and looked for Kellach and Moyra.

"Stupid!" Driskoll said to himself when he saw them sitting at a table in a far corner off to his right, with Breddo. "I must have missed them when I first came in!"

He quickly made his way to their table and flung himself into an empty chair.

Kellach smirked. "Well, it's about time. Finally got up the courage to open the door, huh?"

Driskoll crossed his arms. "No . . . I thought you went in the back and—hey? What's wrong?"

Moyra's face was as red as an apple, and her fists were bunched up on her thighs. Breddo's head was bowed over his tankard of ale.

"What? What happened?" Driskoll asked. "What did I miss?"

"Kellach, could you do the honors?" Moyra said between tightly clenched teeth. Driskoll felt the tiny hairs on the back of his neck begin to rise.

"Kellach? What is it?"

Kellach waved his hand toward Breddo. "Breddo was just telling us about the medallion."

Something hard fell in Driskoll's stomach. "How does Breddo know about that?"

"Because, little brother, it wasn't Royma who stole the medallion. It was Breddo."

5

Driskoll's jaw dropped. "What?"

"That's right." Kellach nodded. "It was Breddo, not Royma."

Driskoll turned to Moyra. She looked more than shocked. She looked crestfallen.

Finally, she found the strength to speak.

"Daddy, I don't understand." Moyra gripped the arms of the chair tightly. "Mom said she found the medallion buried in the yard."

"Yes," Breddo said quietly, without looking up. "You see, I hid it there."

"Dad!" Moyra buried her face in her hands. "How could you!"

Kellach placed a hand on her arm for a second. Then he drilled Breddo with one of his most serious glares. "Sir, I don't mean to be presumptuous here, but perhaps you had better start from the beginning."

Breddo sighed and wrapped his hand more tightly around the tankard. "I suppose you're right, of course." He stared at Moyra.

"But I swear I had no idea that taking the pretty thing would lead your mother into trouble. And that's the truth. It was just that the medallion was so pretty. And it seemed to call out to me, it did. I just had to have it. I just had to. I didn't mean for any of this to happen." Breddo took a sip from his mug and licked his lips, then he looked back pleadingly at Moyra. "Honest, my darling. You must believe me."

"Sir," Kellach tried again, "when did you first see the medallion?"

"Mind you, I didn't see it, not at first. At first I had only heard about it. In prison, that is. One of my visits to that grand establishment."

Breddo chuckled, but the three sitting around him did not crack a smile.

"Ahem. Anyway, now, there was this old feller in one of the cells. He kept talking about this medallion that he'd found. He kept bragging about it, saying how wonderful it was, how beautiful it was, going on and on. The rest of us, well, we would tell him to shut right up. Tired of listening to him, we were. But this feller, he would just laugh. And not a kindly laugh, no, not a nice laugh at all, don't you know. It was a nasty laugh, I tell you."

"Lexos," Kellach, Moyra, and Driskoll said together.

"Yes, Lexos, that's the name," Breddo confirmed. "The old town magistrate, if I recall. He caused a bit of trouble a while back."

A bit of trouble, Driskoll thought. Talk about an understatement!

"So how did you get your hands on the medallion?" Kellach asked.

"It happened the day I was released from prison. I was just leaving my own cell, when I saw an arm dangling between the bars of another cell. And there it was—the medallion. Dangling from its chain, right in front of my own eyes. I froze, I tell you, at the sight of it. So pretty, it was! With a bloomin' bird, or something with wings, carved into it. And a pair of wondrous purple eyes."

Driskoll noted Breddo's star-struck gaze, as if he'd just seen his first sword or something. Driskoll rolled his eyes for Moyra and Kellach's benefit.

But they were not amused.

"I probably would have stared at such a treasure forever," Breddo went on, "if a watcher hadn't yanked me up the stairs. I was signing my papers to be released, and I saw it—the arm."

"The arm?" Driskoll repeated.

"Yes, the arm. You see, I thought I recognized the old robe that had poked between the bars. And there he stood by the duty desk—the old town magistrate, Lexos. As the fates would have it, Lexos and I had both been let out at the same time. Well, I thought to myself. Now how is that for being interesting?"

"Don't tell me," Moyra said, shaking her head. "You followed him, didn't you?"

"Why, of course! I don't think he even knew I was there. I followed him to a small hut at the edge of Curston. Not much to speak of, really. Nicer than the prison, that's for sure, but probably not as nice as when he'd been magistrate. To think that—"

"What did you do next?" Moyra said, trying to keep her father on track.

"Oh, right." Breddo took a gulp from his tankard. "Well, I

sat outside his window, don't you know, and I watched him move about for a while. He seemed rather bothered, really. Kept pacing and muttering, he did."

"What about the medallion?" Kellach persisted.

"Yes, I'm getting to that. After a bit of time, Lexos went out again. I saw him slip the medallion into his pocket. So I followed him back into Curston proper."

"And let me guess," Moyra said, once again shaking her head. "When the time was right, you bumped into him and picked his pocket."

"That's my girl!" Breddo beamed. "Knows her old daddy like, well, like she knows her old daddy!"

"And then you buried the medallion in our yard," Moyra finished for him.

"Indeed I did. Safest place. Or so I thought." Breddo's grin faded. "I didn't think that your old mom would unearth it. And now it's her they've locked up, isn't it?" Breddo's expression saddened briefly, then brightened. "But she'll soon be home, won't she? After all, she didn't steal the medallion. Holding it isn't the same as stealing it, is it?"

"It's much more serious than that, sir," Kellach said. "Lexos wants your wife to be severely punished for the crime. Our father told us that Lexos claims the medallion is very valuable, and that the punishment should match that value."

"What are you saying, lad?"

"Dad—" Moyra gulped, but she couldn't continue.

"We have a plan, sir," Driskoll spoke up. No use getting Breddo all worked up, he decided. It would just distract Breddo from what they really needed.

31

"A plan?"

"Yes, sir," Driskoll went on when Kellach and Moyra stared at him. "Um, well, we thought if we could give the medallion back to Lexos, we could exchange it for Royma's freedom."

"How splendid!" Breddo exclaimed. "Aren't you the clever ones, eh?"

"The only trouble, sir, is that the medallion is being kept at the treasury," Driskoll said.

This news seemed to deflate Breddo as nothing had before. "The treasury?"

"Yes, sir," Driskoll said. "And we were thinking, sir, that with your, er, knowledge, you could help us break into the treasury and get the medallion back."

"Impossible," Breddo said.

"Excuse me?" Kellach said.

"The treasury, lad. It's not possible to break into that place." Breddo lifted his mug for one final swallow, draining it of every last drop. He placed the empty mug on the table with a solid thump, then wiped his mouth with his sleeve.

"Sir, I don't think you realize—" Driskoll started.

"No, lad, you don't realize," Breddo said. "The room where they keep confiscated treasure is guarded by more than just watchers. It's guarded by a terrible, horrible beastie called an ormyrr."

"An ormyrr?" Driskoll repeated.

Breddo nodded. "One of the most disgusting creatures I've ever seen in my life. Like a giant slug, you see, but over twenty feet long. Rows of sharp, pointed teeth. Devilish red eyes." Breddo shivered. "Even if you can manage to get past the watchers, you'll never get past the ormyrr. Not only is the ormyrr horrible and fierce, it is also extremely intelligent. There's no fooling that beastie, that's for sure."

Driskoll looked around the table at the glum faces of his companions. He'd had enough of talking and discussing. He was ready for some action.

"We can do it!" he said, standing from his chair, his hand grasping the hilt of his sword. "We've faced worse. We'll figure this out. Maybe one of Zendric's books has some information on the ormyrr, like that book I found this morning—"

"Yes!" Kellach said, standing up and joining his brother, his blond hair flowing around his shoulders. "*A Practical Guide to Monsters*. The ormyrr works at the treasury. You can't get more practical than that. The creature must be listed in there."

"Which means that the book probably has information on how to defeat him!" Driskoll finished.

Now it was Moyra's turn to jump up. "Let's go!"

"I'd try to talk you and your friends out of facing the beastie, but I can see that you've made up your minds." Breddo smiled briefly. "Just like your old man, eh?"

Despite how angry she was with him, Moyra leaned down and kissed her father on the forehead. "Let us know if you think of anything else, okay?"

Moyra straightened, and the trio dashed from the Skinned Cat, barging back onto the streets of Broken Town. They half ran, half walked through the winding alleys, which eventually led to the nicer parts of Curston. As they approached Zendric's tower, the sun was just setting, casting the building in an eerie amber glow.

Kellach, Driskoll, and Moyra rushed through the door and clamored up the steps.

"Zendric! Zendric!" Kellach called. "We have news!"

"So do I, Kellach," Zendric said as he appeared at the door, his dark robes flowing regally around him. "And none of it is good."

CHAPTER

6

"So Lexos has been freed," Zendric said calmly as he settled into his chair.

The group was clustered around the fieldstone fireplace. Driskoll felt like his heart was about to jump out of his chest. And his stomach had a queasy feeling, like he'd just eaten something rotten. He nervously paced around the room.

"You sound like you expected it," Kellach said.

Driskoll glanced at his brother. Kellach kept brushing his hair off his forehead, a sign that Kellach was full of nervous energy himself.

"I had sensed that something foul had been unleashed, but I wasn't sure what, exactly, it was." Zendric leaned back in his chair and drummed his fingers along its padded arms. "When Moyra whisked you off this afternoon, I began to straighten up the books that Driskoll saw fit to scatter about the room."

Moyra, who was also nervously pacing the room, gave Driskoll a sharp glance.

"It was an accident," Driskoll whispered.

"One of the books had been at the bottom of the pile, for it was the largest and one of the oldest." Zendric paused. "The book lay open, as if someone had flipped the pages, yet I don't recall Driskoll having perused this particular tome. I picked up the book to see what had been revealed." Zendric indicated the large book in his lap. "This is that book, and these are the pages to which the book had mysteriously opened."

Kellach leaned over the chair, and Moyra and Driskoll gathered around the wizard to peer over his shoulder.

Kellach was the first to realize the significance. "A medallion!"

"Not just any medallion," Zendric went on. "The medallion of the silver dragon."

"I didn't know we had a medallion!" Driskoll said, getting excited. "Is it magic or something?"

"Indeed it is when held in the hands of an experienced wizard. Or a cleric, like Lexos."

"What are its powers?" Kellach asked.

Zendric rubbed his chin. "The medallion has the power to entrance people."

"Entrance," Driskoll said thoughtfully. "You mean, like, hypnotize them?"

Moyra snapped her fingers. "That makes sense! That's what my father said, remember? He said that he couldn't take his eyes off the medallion. And my mom also claimed that it was hard for her to look away from it. Let me see that picture."

Zendric held the book up higher.

"That's it!" Moyra shouted. "My father described the medallion as having a bird carved into it with purple eyes."

"It's not a bird," Kellach began.

"It's a silver dragon!" Driskoll finished for him.

Driskoll walked around the chair and squatted on Zendric's right, staring at the page. "But I thought silver dragons were good and peaceful. Why would the silver dragons make a medallion that would hypnotize people?"

"The medallion was used long ago to calm fierce warriors and monsters. The medallion, when gazed upon, creates an amazing feeling. It forces one to avoid conflict. It makes one wish to please others."

"So the medallion doesn't make people do evil things," Driskoll said. "Just the opposite. It makes them peaceful."

Everyone was silent for a moment as they absorbed this information. Then Kellach shouted suddenly, "Dad!"

"Dad?" Driskoll said.

"Yes, Dad!" Kellach leaned forward. "Remember how we thought Dad was acting strangely at the news that Lexos had been released? How he didn't think it was a big deal? How he kept insisting that Lexos had changed?"

"Right," Driskoll said slowly.

"It's the medallion! Lexos probably used it to calm Dad's objections to his release."

Driskoll nodded. "It makes more sense than to think that Dad had lost his mind."

"In a way, Driskoll," Zendric said, "If Torin had been under the spell of the medallion, you could say that he had lost his mind."

Driskoll slumped back on his heels. "So if the medallion has the power to hypnotize people, how are we supposed to get our hands on it, without being hypnotized ourselves?"

Zendric folded his hands in his lap. "Only someone with a wizard's or a high cleric's powers can touch the medallion without it having any effect."

"I get it," Moyra said, scrambling around Driskoll and sitting on the floor in front of Zendric. "That's why Lexos was able to handle it. Because he was once a cleric."

"So that means that you'll have to get it from the treasury?" Driskoll asked.

Zendric smiled. "I'm too old to break into buildings and face ormyrrs. You three are more than capable of completing the task."

"But you said—" Driskoll began.

Zendric snapped his gaze at Driskoll. "I said that someone with a wizard's powers, could handle the medallion."

All eyes turned slowly to Kellach.

"Yes, Kellach. Obtaining the medallion of the silver dragon is your quest. You, and only you can claim it and return it to its rightful owner."

Kellach sat up straighter. "Certainly, I can do that!"

Driskoll shook his head. "Wait a minute. Its rightful owner?"

Zendric eyed each of them in turn. Then he said, "The medallion must be returned to the silver dragon who made it."

Moyra sighed. "Okay, I've been able to follow all this stuff about magic medallions and wizard's powers and whatever else. But we still haven't solved the main problem here. What about my mother?"

Everyone at the table, Zendric included, blinked at her.

Moyra sat forward. "I mean, if we can't return the medallion to Lexos, then how are we going to trade the medallion for my mother's freedom?" Her voice went up at the end with a note of panic, and she blushed.

Driskoll didn't blame her. Although Driskoll and Kellach's mother had disappeared years ago, and no one knew where she was, the hole she had left in their lives was sometimes hard to overcome. Driskoll could understand Moyra's panicky feeling at possibly losing her mom.

Zendric snapped the book shut and stood. "We'll have to make a replacement,"

"A replacement? Is that possible?" Moyra looked up at him hopefully.

"It's not only possible, it's imperative," Zendric said. "Lexos must not be given the real medallion. Otherwise he will use it for his own evil purposes. While you are stealing the real medallion from the treasury, I will stay here and begin to work on the fake medallion. I'll reference the books we have here to get the exact size to get us started. But we'll need the real medallion to get all the details exactly right. Then we will face Lexos. Together."

"You'd be willing to go with us?" Driskoll asked. "After all Lexos did to you?"

"I have to face my old adversary sometime," Zendric said. "It might as well be now."

Driskoll cleared his throat. "We still have one problem."

"What might that be?" Zendric raised an eyebrow.

"How are we supposed to break into the treasury and beat the ormyrr?"

39

CHAPTER

7

"Do you really think this is going to work?" Driskoll whispered the following morning as they sat on a bench in the plaza, staring at the treasury.

Built of solid marble blocks, the building loomed over the street, twice as tall as the structures on either side. The bright, white stones of its face stood out against the crumbling gray bricks of the buildings surrounding it. Completed only one year ago, the treasury was Curston's newest civic building. The original structure had been burned to the ground five years earlier in the wake of the evil that emerged from the Sundering of the Seal.

Stone gargoyles—hideous creatures with bulging eyes, pointed ears, and wicked smiles—had been sculpted and attached to the building's façade at irregular intervals. Two of the largest watchers Driskoll had ever seen stood guard outside the building's massive marble door.

"Of course it will work," Kellach replied. "We talked it over with Zendric until curfew last night. And I didn't hear you coming up with any better ideas."

"It's just . . ." Driskoll gulped. "Breaking into the treasury is serious. If we're caught, not even Dad can get us out of it. What if they decide to check out our story?"

"We've gone over this a million times," Kellach hissed back. "We're not going to get caught."

"Yeah, but I still think—"

"Will you two give it a rest?" Moyra said. "We're running out of time as it is. My mom only has one day and one night left before—"

Moyra bit her lip to stop herself from saying anything more.

Kellach pulled a small white bundle from his pocket and unwrapped it. Glancing down, Driskoll saw the crystal prism from one of Zendric's shelves.

Driskoll felt sweat drip down his neck, even though the morning was cool. "You really think the watchers are going to believe that that prism is so valuable, that it has to be kept in the treasury."

"Trust me," Kellach said. "Watchers are not experts when it comes to magical devices. They have no way to know whether it's valuable or not."

"I still think we should have taken something bigger," Driskoll said. "Something more convincing."

"It's not the item that will be convincing," Kellach said, repeating words they'd heard throughout the night from Zendric. "But us who will have to do the convincing."

Moyra suddenly leaped from the bench. "I've had enough of this! Let's just do it." Without looking back, she strode across the street and began mounting the stairs.

"Halt!" The watchers held out their spears to prevent Moyra from entering.

"She's nuts!" Driskoll said, bolting up from the bench and going after her.

"No, just desperate," Kellach said as they rushed up the stairs.

"I told you," Moyra yelled at the watchers. "I've come with the captain's sons. We have something to drop off." She shot a look over her shoulder, just as Driskoll and Kellach reached her side. "See? Here they are now."

Driskoll had to lift his head to meet the gaze of the watchers.

Kellach grabbed the end of one spear and thrust it aside. "How dare you pull a weapon on us!"

"You the captain's sons?" growled the watcher whose spear had been touched.

"Would we be coming to the treasury if we were not?" Kellach said.

The other watcher spat a hefty gob at their feet. He did not lower his spear. "That depends on your business here."

Kellach reached into the pouch at his side. Driskoll saw the watchers tighten their grips on their spears. "I have an item of value that our father—your captain—has asked us to transport to the treasury for safekppeing."

"A transportation?" The watcher narrowed his eyes. "I don't recall receiving information about a transportation this morning."

"It was very sudden," Kellach continued in that same formal, confident tone. "We were having breakfast with our father at Watchers' Hall, when this item arrived on his desk. He asked that we bring it here straight away."

The watcher ran a hand through his beard, the spear still raised. "Hmm. I know Torin has sons, but I've never met them." Jerking his head to indicate Moyra, he said, "Who's she?"

"This is our friend, Moyra. She was with us at breakfast this morning, and we didn't see any harm in letting her accompany us on this official task."

The watcher still looked skeptical. "Let me see this object that is so valuable."

Kellach shook his head and smiled, stuffing the wrapped bundle back into his pouch. "My good man, you don't expect us to reveal the valuable here, out of doors, where anyone might come along and snatch it out of our hands? My father would be very angry with us if we failed."

The watcher slowly lowered his spear, and his companion did the same. "Hmm. All right, go on in, then." He opened the door.

Kellach, Moyra, and Driskoll threw each other relieved glances.

"Phynkin!" the watcher boomed into the dark opening of the treasury door.

They waited only a moment, and then a dwarf, dressed in a watcher's uniform, waddled to the door. "Yar? What is it?"

"We have visitors this morning," the watcher announced. "Official messengers from Torin."

"Yar? And what might they officially be doing here?"

"It's a transportation," the watcher said. "And Phynkin—take good care of our messengers. They're Torin's sons."

"Tor-Torin's sons, you say? Well, how about that! Come in. Come in."

Driskoll watched Kellach bow to the spear-wielding watchers and to the dwarf, Phynkin, before following him inside.

Be convincing! Be convincing! Driskoll said to himself as he, too, entered the treasury. The door shut behind them with an ominous boom.

Step one was now complete. They were inside the treasury. Now for step two.

The threesome followed the dwarf as he wobbled down the dark hallway. Fire-lit sconces hung from the walls every few feet to brighten the dark space. He led them to a room in which several watchers, both human and dwarf, were still eating a breakfast of fresh fruits, shanks of meat, cheese, and bread.

"Well," Phynkin said, turning his attention to the children. "Let's see the transportation, then."

Kellach pulled the wrapped bundle from his pouch and removed the crystal prism.

"Hmph," Phynkin said, obviously not impressed. "I don't see what's so special about it."

Kellach shrugged. "I don't either, sir. I'm just following through on what our father asked us to do."

"Fine," the dwarf muttered, ambling over to a desk. "Let me just find the forms to fill out and—"

"Oh, no!" Driskoll moaned, on cue. "Where did Moyra go?"

The dwarf looked up from his task. "The girl?"

Kellach shook his head and smiled apologetically. "Happens all the time. She's not quite right in the head, you see." Kellach looked over his shoulder at his brother. "Driskoll, go find her, will you?"

Driskoll gave his brother a mock salute, then headed out the door after Moyra. He found her waiting, just outside the door, hiding in the shadows.

"It's been too easy so far," Moyra whispered.

"I know!" Driskoll said. "Let's see if Kellach can finagle his way out of there now."

Driskoll and Moyra listened to the watchers in the other room. They held back a few nervous giggles as the watchers emitted more burps. Then they heard Kellach speak. "If you don't mind, sir. While you're filling out those forms, I must use your facilities."

"Fine, fine," grumbled the dwarf. "Just make it quick."

"I'll only be a moment," Kellach said. "I'm sure my father will be most happy to hear how accommodating you've been."

Driskoll could just imagine the stout dwarf pushing out his chest. "Er, why, thank you. Kellach, did you say?"

Kellach's shadow appeared in the doorway. "Yes, sir. I'll only be a moment. Thank you so much."

He was practically bowing his way out backward, when Driskoll grabbed him by his robes and dragged him to their hiding spot.

"Let's go!" he whispered. "Before they realize that all three of us are missing."

Kellach and Moyra didn't need further prompting. Moyra had already pulled out a map from her boot. After studying it, she began to lead the boys down a number of nondescript hallways that twisted and turned and took them deeper into the bowels of the treasury.

The farther they went, the warmer the air became, until it was stifling hot and humid. The air smelled mossy, like they were deep underground. Driskoll felt the sweat roll down his back and prickle along his neck.

He could see the sweat beading on Kellach's brow as well. Only Moyra seemed unaffected by the warmth.

"Are you sure you're reading that thing right?" Driskoll whispered as he loosened the collar around his neck. "It sure is getting hot in here."

"Of course!" Moyra said, irritated. "I can read a map."

"We've been walking forever. It can't be that far," Driskoll insisted.

"It's not much farther," Moyra hissed.

A few twists and a bunch more turns later, and they found themselves before a large metal door.

"This is it." Moyra rolled the map back up and stuffed it back into her boot. "You boys ready to meet an ormyrr?"

As if in answer, a roar came from inside the door.

CHAPTER

8

Moyra put her hand on the latch on the door. It moved easily beneath her fingers.

"I can't believe they don't lock this place," she said. "Why should they?" Kellach pointed out. "After all, they've got a twenty-five-foot worm in there, standing guard."

"Standing?" Driskoll said, trying to make a joke. "Can worms stand?"

"Well, we're about to find out," Moyra said. And with one last big breath, she pushed the door forward.

"Holy potatoes!" Moyra screamed.

"Potatoes?" Driskoll said as he peered over Moyra's shoulder. "What do potatoes have to do with—"

And that's when he saw it.

An enormous slug stretched the entire length of the room, from wall to wall. The height of its wormlike body rose above them like a blue slimy wall. It had a million feathery feet, like those of a centipede, and four arms that held a spear-like weapon.

47

It was definitely the ormyrr. Driskoll recognized it from its picture in A *Practical Guide to Monsters.*

But the drawing in the book didn't capture the putrid blue of the monster's skin or the glowing redness of its fierce eyes. The drawing didn't include drops of spit that hung from the creature's fanged teeth. And it didn't show how the tip of its spear gleamed across its razor-sharp edge.

The slug's body blocked most of the treasures in the room, but Driskoll could see the tops of several mounds behind it, mounds of gold coins, ornate chalices, and chests studded with gems.

As he scanned the mounds of treasure, Driskoll's heart sank. The collection of valuables didn't seem to have any organization. Looking for the medallion would be like searching for a fairy's tooth among a million dandelion seeds.

Driskoll groaned. "How are we ever going to—"

Driskoll's words were cut off by an enormous eruption from the ormyrr. The ormyrr lifted its head, which nearly touched the ceiling of the cave-like room, opened its hideous mouth, and let go a deafening, hair-lifting roar. Then it lowered its head and peered at them, its black-blue eyebrows—or what Driskoll thought were eyebrows—beetling over its eyeballs. And its breath! Driskoll tried hard not to gag. The ormyrr had a stench like it had just gulped an entire pig-sty's worth of rotten eggs.

"I think he's angry," Moyra pronounced.

Driskoll pulled his sword from its scabbard and gripped it tightly. "What makes you think it's a he?"

"You're right," Moyra reconsidered. "I take it back!"

The ormyrr roared again, and this time it lunged, the upper part of its body flinging toward them. Its jaws snapped, and its thin arms raised against its body, the spear waving in the air.

Kellach, Moyra, and Driskoll scattered about the room, trying to draw its attention away from the treasures that it guarded. Driskoll could just make out the gleam of gold and silver behind the ormyrr's bulbous body.

"Kellach!" he shouted. "Whatever you're going to do, do it fast! And now!"

As Driskoll watched, Kellach raised his arms slowly, chanting all the while. His voice sounded steady and strong, unlike Driskoll's shout, which had sounded wobbly, even to his own ears.

In front of the ormyrr, a small whirlwind began to appear. Air and dust twirled and sparkled, growing and churning. It spun more quickly and more fantastically, a blur of color and flashing streams of light. The whirlwind lifted higher, higher, until it twirled right before the monster's eyes. It was a kaleidoscope of pinks and blues and purples and golds, all shimmering and dancing in the air.

Driskoll glanced at the creature, who still looked menacing, but now also looked, well, *curious.* As he stared, the creature's mouth began to lift into—could it be? Yes! It lifted into a smile.

"I think it's working!" Driskoll shouted, his sword arm still raised.

When they had been at Zendric's, they'd read the entire entry about ormyrrs, and they'd discovered the ormyrr's weakness. It wasn't its slimy, blue skin, or its ferocious red eyes.

No, the ormyrr's weakness was magic. The creatures were fascinated by it. Although they had no magical ability of their own, ormyrrs's greatest ambition was to become magic-users themselves.

"I told you it would work!" Driskoll called out again. Kellach smiled briefly, but didn't take his eyes off the ormyrr or the whirlwind of colors he was creating.

With the ormyrr distracted for the moment, Driskoll turned his attention to Moyra. "Have you found it?"

"I'm looking, I'm looking!" He heard her scrambling behind the worm. "This place is so unorganized! Everything's just piled up back here."

By this time, the ormyrr had dropped its spear, and all four hands were clapping. It sounded like someone slapping together two very large pairs of soggy, wet boots.

"Hurry, Moyra! I don't think Kellach can keep it up much longer."

Suddenly Moyra appeared around the tail end of the ormyrr. "Eureka!" she cried, holding up a nondescript burlap sack. "They must have put it in this ugly bag so it wouldn't attract attention."

"Or hypnotize anyone!" Driskoll shouted. "Come on!"

Driskoll and Moyra ran toward Kellach, who still stood near the entrance. Dodging behind him, they ran back through the doorway, pausing in the entrance. Kellach, with a particularly dramatic flourish of his arms, dispersed the whirling dust into a splattering of starry figures that twinkled and then vanished.

By the time the last twinkle had disappeared, Kellach was through the door himself.

Moyra pulled the door shut, trapping the ormyrr inside.

"Do you think the ormyrr realizes what we did?" Driskoll asked, as he leaned against the door panting.

A thunderous roar answered that question.

"Let's not wait to see what he'll do when he's really angry," Kellach said as he took off down the hall.

"Wait!" Moyra shouted after him. "I thought we'd decided he was a she."

"Whatever!" Driskoll said. "Let's just be grateful that the door doesn't have a handle on the inside. I'd hate to think of that thing chasing us down the halls, especially since we're not sure exactly how to get out of here."

"That's right!" Moyra hopped forward, as she pulled the rolled-up map from her boot. "Kellach, wait! Let's make sure we're going the right way."

Kellach slowed and waited for his brother and Moyra to catch up to him. "So how do we get out of here?"

Handing over the burlap sack with the medallion to Kellach, Moyra studied the map for a few moments. "I think I've got it," Moyra said. She traced a path on the map, indicating the reverse direction from which they'd come. "Worst case, we'll just have to backtrack and—"

A roar echoed down the hall.

"I'm not backtracking!" Driskoll shouted as he took off at a run. "You just better be right!" He barreled down the corridor in the direction Moyra had indicated.

The trek back through the treasury was just as long and winding as it had been when they'd entered. Finally, they could hear voices and belches, and they knew they were near the room in which the watchers relaxed.

Now all they had to do was creep by the room and make it to the front door.

As Driskoll squared his shoulders and prepared to move, he heard the words they'd all been dreading.

"Hey! Where are you kids going?"

CHAPTER

9

Kellach, Moyra, and Driskoll turned slowly. Phynkin stood in the doorway, his stubby arms perched on his hips. His face looked more perplexed than angry.

"Don't you boys have something to drop off for your father?" he asked.

Kellach stepped forward. "Yes, sir!"

"Well, don't dawdle, boy. I'm a busy watcher. We have things to do today." The dwarf turned around in a huff and walked back to the main room.

"I was hoping he'd just forget about us," Driskoll said, running a hand through his hair. "Guess we'll have to turn over Zendric's prism, huh?"

"No," Kellach said, drawing out the word.

"What are you talking about?" asked Moyra. "If we don't leave the prism behind, they'll be suspicious."

Kellach's eyes held a faraway look, and Driskoll groaned. "Kellach, what are you thinking?"

"What I'm thinking," said Kellach, "is that we're going to

54

see if this thing really works."

"What?" Moyra and Driskoll both shouted. They didn't have time to ask Kellach what he was babbling about. At that moment, Phynkin appeared in the doorway again.

"Are you coming or aren't you?" he said, tapping his foot.

"Coming," said Kellach. He strode forward, his head held high, a slight swagger to his step. Driskoll shook his head and followed his brother into the room, with Moyra close behind.

Kellach produced the burlap sack from beneath his robes. Holding the sack in one hand, Kellach untied the string that bound the top together. He pulled forth the medallion, with the silver dragon engraved upon its surface. The medallion glinted in the firelight from the torches and the candles that lit the room.

Driskoll stared at the medallion, his gaze transfixed. The purple jewels of the dragon's eyes seemed to stare into his own, and the dragon's smile made Driskoll smile back. Driskoll found that he wanted to grant the dragon anything, do anything the dragon asked. Moyra hadn't said a word since Kellach had pulled out the medallion, so Driskoll sensed that she, too, must feel the pull of the medallion's powers.

Kellach turned his back to them, and their view of the medallion broke. And so did the spell.

"Whoa!" Driskoll said so only Moyra could hear him. "Did you feel that?"

"I did!" Moyra said. "It was like I was being sucked in by it or something."

"Or something is right," Driskoll agreed, shaking his head to clear it. "And look! I think the medallion is having the same effect on our little dwarf friend there."

Driskoll pointed to Phynkin, who stared at the medallion dangling from its chain. Phynkin's eyes looked glassy and his lips tilted up in a silly smile. The papers he'd completed still lay in a neat pile on his desk.

In fact, none of the watchers uttered a sound. No belching or throat-clearing or munching. Nothing. Driskoll realized they'd all stopped what they'd been doing to gaze at the medallion.

"Do you know what?" Kellach said, as if it had just occurred to him. "I think I made a mistake. I think my father wanted me to take this valuable to the vault at Watchers' Hall, not to the treasury."

"Watchers' Hall?" Phynkin repeated, his gaze still glued to the dangling circle of silver.

"Yes, Watchers' Hall." Kellach stared intently at the dwarf. "So, we'll just be off. No need to contact Torin. We'll be fine."

"Fine," Phynkin repeated. "You'll be fine."

"Yes," Kellach said. He began to back away. He edged toward the doorway and stood directly in front of Driskoll and Moyra. Driskoll still couldn't see the medallion.

"And you won't mention this to Torin," Kellach said one last time.

"No. No need to bother the captain," Phynkin agreed.

"Good," Kellach said. He whipped the medallion up by its chain, grasped the silver piece, and placed it back in the burlap sack.

One of the watchers let out an extremely large burp.

Driskoll held his breath to see what would happen next. One by one, the other watchers swung their heads from side to side, as if looking for something. Seeing only the children in the doorway, they began to laugh uproariously.

"That was a good one, Ebbett!" one watcher said to the dwarf who had belched so gloriously.

"Thank you!" Ebbett responded, blushing. "I've been practicing."

"I guess the spell is broken," Driskoll whispered to Kellach.

"Looks like it," Kellach said.

"Come on!" Moyra urged, pulling on both their sleeves. "What's with you two? Are you hypnotized by the magical powers of a burp?" She dragged them into the hallway and out the treasury door.

The sun sparkled above, and people scurried along the sidewalk, going about their business as if it were any other day. A horse clopped by slowly, its head bobbing up and down as it pulled a cart, loaded with blankets.

"We did it!" Moyra said, as she bounced down the marble steps. "We really did it!"

"I can't believe you tried the medallion on the watchers," Driskoll said, crossing his arms and glaring at his brother. "I mean, that could have been a disaster."

Kellach shrugged and threw up his arms. "Not with a wizard like me controlling it." A wide grin grew on his face. "Those watchers stared at the medallion like it was the most precious object in the world."

"I felt the same way," Moyra said, "when I looked at it."

"Me too," Driskoll said. "But seriously, Kellach. That medallion is dangerous. What if it had turned you evil, like Lexos? Did you feel anything?"

Kellach bit his lip and looked up. "A sense of power, maybe. But it wasn't overwhelming. Remember? Zendric said that the power the medallion wields is in proportion to the powers of the person who holds it." Kellach paused. "Of course, my powers, for an apprentice, are quite impressive."

Driskoll looked at Moyra and rolled his eyes.

"What?" Kellach glanced at his brother. "Even Zendric says so."

"Your powers were enough for today, and that's all that matters." Moyra pulled Kellach by the arm. "We still have a lot to do. And not much time. We only have twenty-four hours left. Now, come on!"

■ ■ ▮ ■ ▮

Soon they were back at Zendric's tower. They gathered around the worktable, and Kellach carefully pulled out the burlap sack from the pocket inside his robes. He removed the medallion and let the silver circle rest in the palm of his hand.

Zendric leaned in, eyed it closely, then sighed. "It's been a long while since I've seen a silver dragon medallion. I thought they'd all been destroyed during the Sundering of the Seal. I never thought I'd see another one again."

Zendric turned to Kellach. "What do you feel, Kellach, when you look at it?"

"I don't feel anything in my head, if that makes any sense," Kellach said. "I don't feel like I'm being affected by it. But I feel like a twinge or a shock in the palm of my hand."

Zendric gingerly lifted the medallion from Kellach's palm. "Very good, very good."

Kellach grinned and poked his brother. "See! I told you! Even Zendric says I'm good."

"I said no such thing," Zendric added without taking his eyes off the silver circlet. "You still have much to learn."

Kellach shrugged his shoulders and Driskoll and Moyra couldn't help but giggle.

Zendric raised the medallion to his eyes and studied it closely. "Such fine craftsmanship. Such delicate work. The silver dragon who made this was very noble, indeed."

Moyra hopped up on the work table to get a better look. "You can tell that by looking at it?" she asked, swinging her legs back and forth.

"Yes," said Zendric. "The detailing is very precise, very intricate. Only a dragon could craft such a beautiful piece. It will not be easy to duplicate."

Moyra's legs stopped swinging. "But you *can* duplicate, right?"

"It will take time," Zendric said solemnly.

"But we don't have time!" Moyra jumped off the table. "My mom doesn't have time!"

"It's okay, Moyra," Kellach said.

"No, it's not okay! What if Zendric can't make a fake one? What if all this sneaking into the treasury was a huge waste of time? What if they hang my mom anyway?"

Moyra slammed her hand against the table and glared at Kellach, then at Driskoll, and finally at Zendric. "Well? What if?"

Zendric calmly picked up the burlap sack from the table and placed the medallion inside. Then he smiled at Moyra. "It will be done," he said.

Moyra threw her hands in the air. "When?"

"In time, my dear, in time." Zendric folded his arms inside the long sleeves of his robes, the burlap sack disappearing along with them. "I have arranged with your parents that you will be sleeping here. Now come with me. We have a long night ahead of us."

⬥ ⬥ ⬥ ⬥ ⬥

A soft sound jolted Driskoll from a deep sleep.

He wasn't sure what he'd heard, but it had been enough to send a chill down his back and his heart racing.

Driskoll sat up on the soft pallet of blankets beside the fireplace in Zendric's workroom. Zendric had worked well into the evening and had finally completed the fake medallion just before midnight. Now the real medallion lay in a safe place in Zendric's tower, while the fake medallion had been wrapped up in the burlap sack that they'd taken from the treasury.

The magical resources required to create a truly convincing duplicate had been enormous, even more so than Zendric had imagined. By the end of the evening, Zendric had been so weakened by the spell, he could barely stand, and Driskoll and Kellach had to help the old wizard into bed. Moyra was beside herself with worry, but Kellach assured her that after a full night's rest, the wizard would be back to normal. Then, he promised, they'd go see Lexos. Together.

Driskoll stretched and peered into the darkness. He didn't see anything out of the ordinary. The smoldering embers in the fireplace gave off a dull glow. Through the window, he could see the dark night outside. Humps ranged around the room, and although they could be anything, Driskoll knew they were just furniture of Zendric's workroom—the long table, the chairs, the stacks of books. The lump to his right was Kellach. And the lump to his left—

"Moyra!" Driskoll flung back his blankets and sprang up. He walked quickly around the room, checking each corner, each hiding place.

Driskoll rushed back to his pallet and knelt down next to Kellach. "Kell, wake up!"

"Wh-what is it?"

"Sh! I don't want to wake up Zendric! He needs his sleep."

Kellach rolled over and rubbed his eyes. "So what's the matter?"

"It's Moyra. She's gone!"

"What?" Kellach sat up on his elbows.

"She's gone, Kell. And I think she took the fake medallion with her."

CHAPTER

10

"We should have known she would do something like this," said Driskoll.

He and Kellach rushed down the deserted streets of Curston. Early morning was upon them, but no one had yet to venture out. Store doors remained locked, shutters closed, curtains drawn. Every few blocks Driskoll and Kellach passed a stray cat. The hour was still too early for humans.

"We should have suspected that she would take off," said Kellach. "She was so upset last night when I told her we had to wait until morning to confront Lexos."

Driskoll laughed. "Yeah. I thought she was going to throw that wooden owl at you."

Kellach slowed. "I guess we can't blame her. I mean, if it were our mom, I'd probably be just as worried."

Driskoll didn't say anything. He didn't like thinking about their mom. They swiftly walked across town, recalling the directions that Breddo had given them to find Lexos's hut.

Driskoll and Kellach turned down a few more blocks. The sky began to turn from black to a deep gray.

"The sun's coming up," Driskoll said. "Shouldn't we see Lexos's hut by now?"

"There!" Kellach said. He sprinted ahead of Driskoll.

A small hut stood at the end of the dirt road. The hut was no more than four mud walls and a grass-thatched roof. A crude door of wooden planks hung off one hinge. The hut had no windows, and no plants grew in the yard.

The sky began to lighten, and Driskoll saw a slim figure standing in front of the door. Driskoll knew only one person with hair that red.

Moyra!

She flung a glance over her shoulder when she heard Kellach and Driskoll approach. "About time you two showed up."

Driskoll rested his hands on his knees and inhaled deeply. "What are you doing?"

"I'm going to see Lexos," Moyra said. "What does it look like I'm doing?"

Kellach grabbed her arm. "You can't go in there without Zendric."

Moyra glared up at him. "Who says?"

"That was the plan," Driskoll said, straightening.

Moyra shook off Kellach's touch. "No. The plan was to come to Lexos when the medallion was finished, not wait for Zendric to get a good night's sleep."

Kellach placed his hands on her shoulders so she would look at him. "You're cracked! We can't face Lexos without Zendric, and Zendric needs all his strength to face Lexos."

Moyra backed out of Kellach's hands. "All I need is the medallion."

"You can't go in there alone," Kellach insisted.

"I'm not alone!" Moyra marched over to the crude, planked door. "You're here, aren't you?" She planted her feet and raised her fist to knock on the door.

But before her fingers met the rotting wood, the door creaked open.

"Well, well, well," Lexos said. "What do we have here? I expected I might have some visitors, now that I have been released. It never occurred to me that you three would be the first to welcome me back."

Lexos's withered, pruned-up face had more lines, and his head had a few less hairs, but it was definitely the same elf who had tried to kill Zendric. Driskoll could never forget the evil that sparked from his eyes or his sneering smile.

A shabby gray tunic hung loosely on the old elf's body, the sleeves covering his hands, the neck frayed around the edges. Worn brown pants stopped just above his ankles, and a few patches clung to the knees. On his feet he wore sandals, and Driskoll could see smudges of dirt bruising the old magistrate's feet.

Despite his shoddy appearance, Lexos still made Driskoll shiver.

Moyra stepped forward and puffed out her chest. "This isn't the welcome wagon, you big bully. We're here on business."

"Business, you say?" Lexos rasped as he rubbed his hands together. "Well, by all means, young lady, please come in."

Moyra merely nodded. She stepped over the threshold and entered Lexos's hut. Kellach and Driskoll followed.

"It's not much, I'm afraid," Lexos said, waving his arm around the meager furnishings. "But it is home."

Driskoll looked around at the stark interior. A cot with a thin blanket stood against the far wall. A small wooden table sat squarely in the middle of the room, with two chairs set on either side. A fireplace took up the wall to his right, with a black pot of something stewing over the low-burning flames. On the opposite wall sat a low bookshelf, with one large volume the only inhabitant.

"So, children," Lexos said as he sat down on one of the chairs at the table. "To what do I owe the honor of your visit?"

"I think you know," Moyra said evenly. She stood before the old magistrate and peered down at him. "We want you to release my mother."

"Mother?" Lexos said. "Why I didn't know a little upstart like you came with a mother." He lifted a frail, bony hand and massaged his narrow chin. The sight of those long, knobby fingers caused Driskoll to clench his teeth.

"Don't play that game with me. You know who she is," Moyra said. She boldly stepped forward and poked the old elf in the chest. "You've accused her of stealing something that you know she didn't steal."

"Ah, yes! Now I remember her." Lexos slapped his hand on the table. "Royma, is it?"

Moyra glared at him.

Lexos chuckled. "I can see you haven't lost any of your spark, young lady. Still as bold as ever, hmm? And it appears your companions are still as foolish as ever." Lexos leaned forward and eyed Moyra curiously. "What makes you think, my dear, that I give one toad about your mother?"

65

"I don't think you do," Moyra said. "However, I do think you care about something that we have in our possession."

Lexos smiled, mocking her. "And what, pray tell, could you children"—he spat the word—"have that I could ever want?"

Moyra pulled the burlap sack from her jacket pocket. Slowly she began to open it until only the edge of the medallion appeared.

Lexos gasped, and for the first time, Driskoll saw his confidence flicker. "The medallion! It can't be!"

"Oh, but it is," Moyra assured him.

Lexos sat back slowly in his chair. "But it's locked up at the—"

"Treasury?" Moyra continued. "Not anymore. We took it back."

"I don't believe it. No one is allowed access to that vault."

"You underestimated us once, Lexos," Kellach said, joining in the exchange. "Or don't you remember?"

"I remember that you children don't know how to respect your elders!" Lexos shouted.

"We respect those who deserve respect," Kellach said. "Now, do you want to hear what we propose?"

"But how did you—"

"Overcome the ormyrr?" Driskoll said. He slowly removed his sword from its sheath and held it forward. "You've been away a long time, Lexos. Many things have changed."

Lexos narrowed his eyes, making him look even more like a viper. "Are you saying that you slew the ormyrr?"

"Let's just say that he didn't cause us any problems," said Driskoll, his heart beating in his ears. He slid his sword back into its sheath, hoping the cleric hadn't noticed his shaking hand.

Lexos gazed at the three children, one by one. "Perhaps I have been away longer than I thought," he agreed. "Let me hear what you propose, and I'll decide if it's worth it."

Moyra braced her feet. "All we want is my mother."

"Ah! I should have known." Lexos chuckled again and shook his head. "So young, so naïve. You still believe in heroes, don't you?"

"I don't know what you're talking about," Moyra snapped. "All I know is that I want the charges against my mother dropped, and in exchange we'll give you the medallion."

"And Zendric?" Lexos asked.

"What about him?" Kellach said.

"Oh come now, boy! He's your mentor. I'm sure he's had a hand in this."

"You're right, he has," said Kellach. "He told us that you have no power over the medallion. That the medallion only responds to goodness, not to evil."

"Oh, he did, did he?"

"Yes. Therefore, he said it didn't matter to him if you had the medallion or not because it couldn't help you."

Lexos threw back his head and laughed. Driskoll shuddered when he spied the rotting teeth in the old elf's mouth. "You don't expect me to believe that, do you?"

Kellach shrugged.

Lexos narrowed his eyes again and swept his gaze over all three of them. "If this is true, what you say, then why didn't Zendric keep the medallion for himself? Or better yet, give it to you?" He pointed a finger at Kellach. "You are, after all, his apprentice, are you not?"

"I am," said Kellach.

"Then why give the medallion to me?"

"Because I asked him to," Moyra said.

Lexos turned his attention to her. "Hmm. I'm sure you did. Still . . ."

"Look, if it makes you feel any better," Driskoll said, "Zendric put a warding spell on the medallion. It can't do you—or anyone—any good. It's pretty much worthless."

Lexos's lips crooked into a smile. "Yes. Worthless, hmm? Let that old fool believe what he wants. He has no idea of the powers the medallion can bring."

"Look," Moyra said. "I don't care about you or Zendric or that stupid medallion or all the powers in the world. I only care about my mother."

Lexos held out his hand. "Let me see the entire medallion, and then I'll decide."

"Okay," said Moyra. "But don't forget—Zendric put a spell on it. You probably won't feel anything."

"Let me see it!" he ordered.

Moyra pulled the entire medallion out of the burlap. Lexos grabbed it, stood quickly, and walked to the open window. Using the light from the rising sun, he turned the medallion this way and that, exclaiming over one pattern, sighing over another. "It is exquisite."

Kellach snatched the chain out of the old cleric's hand. "You'll have plenty of time for admiring the medallion *after* you give us what we want. " He slipped the silver circlet into his robes and the medallion disappeared from sight.

Lexos sighed. "And, what, pray tell, are the terms of your proposal?"

Kellach's steely gaze never left Lexos's face. "You will accompany us to Watchers' Hall where you will meet with my father personally. After you drop all charges against Royma, I'll give you the medallion."

Lexos raised an eyebrow. "How do I know you will keep your end of the bargain?"

Kellach stepped forward. "Because unlike you, I keep my word."

Lexos chuckled. "Zendric has taught you well, my boy." He walked steadily back to the table and sat down. "I don't usually make bargains, but for old friends like you, I will make an exception."

Moyra inhaled sharply. "You will?"

Driskoll felt the hairs on the back of his neck rise. He didn't know why, but he felt something unexpected was coming.

Lexos leaned his head on one hand. "Losing the medallion has been a great hardship for me, as you know."

"Oh, please!" Moyra said, rolling her eyes.

"Silence!" Lexos slammed his hand on the table. Driskoll saw Moyra wince. "I want someone to pay for my medallion being stolen. Since it is not to be your mother, then how about you?"

He raised his hand from the table and pointed his knobby finger in Moyra's direction.

"Yes, my dear, I think that is a suitable solution." His face broke into a creepy smile. "The mother will be freed. And the daughter will become the prisoner."

CHAPTER

11

No one in the small hut made a sound. The only noise came from the crackling of the fire and a slow drip-drip-drip from somewhere in the room.

Driskoll looked at the stunned faces of his brother and Moyra, and the evil confidence of Lexos.

Kellach finally broke the silence. "No way."

"Pardon?" Lexos said, lifting a sinister brow.

"You heard him, you demented freak!" Driskoll shouted.

Lexos pinched his lips. "You are, indeed, foolish children. I may not be the town magistrate anymore, but I still have considerable power. I think you forget who you are dealing with!"

"I haven't forgotten anything," Kellach said. "And that is exactly why we will never leave Moyra here with you."

Lexos relaxed and began to study his nails. "Fine, then. Leave. I'm bored with you anyway."

Silence descended upon the room.

Finally, Driskoll said, "You don't want the medallion?"

"Bah! Just a silly trinket," said Lexos.

"But that's not what you said a few minutes ago!" Moyra exclaimed. "You can't back out of our deal!"

"I've made you my offer, young lady. Now, you can either accept it or be off."

"Fine!" Moyra stomped her foot. "If it means saving my mom, then I'm staying here."

"No, Moyra, you can't!" Kellach said. "I won't let you."

"You can't tell me what to do," Moyra said. Her green eyes shone brightly when she faced him. Driskoll could see the high patches of color in her cheeks.

Kellach ripped his gaze from Moyra to Lexos. "What do you intend to do with her?"

"Hmm," Lexos said, as he looked Moyra up and down. "I'm not quite sure. I'll have to think about it."

"You can't keep her here forever!" Driskoll said.

"That is not for you to decide," Lexos said, becoming annoyed. "Now, you may leave, or you may go. It makes no difference to me."

"I'll be fine," Moyra said. "Just free my mother. That's all I care about."

"Moyra, no—" Kellach began.

"Don't be a clod. You know I can take care of myself. Go with Lexos and free my mom. I'm counting on you."

"There is another option," Driskoll said sharply.

"Yes?" Lexos smiled.

Driskoll took a deep breath. "I'll stay with her."

"No, Driskoll, you can't!" cried Moyra.

Driskoll lifted his chin. "Of course I can. Lexos didn't say one of us couldn't stay behind with you. I'm volunteering for the job."

Lexos's smile broadened. "Two for the price of one, eh?" He turned to Kellach. "You're awfully quiet, boy apprentice. What do you think of your brother's idea?"

Driskoll drilled Kellach with his glare.

"I think it's a terrible idea," Kellach began, "but it may be the only way." He turned to Driskoll and Moyra. "You're sure—"

"We'll be fine, Kell," Driskoll said. "Besides, you should worry about yourself now, walking through Curston with Lexos."

"I don't think Lexos will try anything out in public." Kellach turned back to Lexos. "Too many witnesses. After all, you have your reputation as the town magistrate to win back."

Lexos thumped his hand on the table and grinned. "My goodness, this is fun. You three don't know when to stop." Then the smile fell into a frown, and his eyes pierced through Kellach's own. "You'll just have to take your chances, boy." He swung his gaze to Driskoll and Moyra. "And that goes for all of you!"

Kellach walked to the door. Turning back, he said to Driskoll and Moyra, "Take care of yourselves."

"You, too, Kell," Driskoll said, his voice a bit shaky. Moyra seemed too moved to speak.

"Touching," Lexos said. "However, just to make sure these two don't get into trouble—" Driskoll watched Lexos sweep away an area of dirt from the floor, revealing a wooden door. "I might as well keep you in a secure place." Lexos leaned down and lifted the door. Driskoll was amazed that Lexos was not as frail as he appeared.

"Well, mistress Moyra?" Lexos asked, as if inviting her to join him for tea. "Would you be so kind as to make yourself comfortable in the room below?"

Moyra bowed slightly. "May I have a candle?"

"Why, of course," Lexos agreed. "No need to be uncivilized."

Moyra walked to the short bookcase and lifted the candle that glowed there. She cast a glance at Lexos and headed for the pit.

"Ahem, aren't you two forgetting something?" Lexos said, holding out his hand.

Driskoll raised his eyebrows.

"Your weapons, children, your weapons! Hand them over."

Moyra removed her knife, while Driskoll slowly unbuckled his belt and handed the sword and scabbard to Lexos. Lexos tossed their things carelessly into a corner, and tapped his toes impatiently, staring at Moyra.

"The lockpicks, too, girl."

Moyra cursed under breath.

"Yes, I know everything about you." Lexos cackled and the sound sent a shiver up Driskoll's spine. "Can't trust the daughter of thieves to go anywhere without lockpicks. Now hand them over."

Driskoll watched Moyra remove her jacket where she kept all her thieving tools, then she bravely lowered herself into the hole in the floor.

He, too, descended into the pit. As Lexos lowered the door and snapped the lock shut, Driskoll cringed at the sound, final and chilling.

"Now, we've wasted enough time," he heard Lexos say to Kellach. "Let's be off."

Driskoll was sure he would never see his brother again.

● ● ▮ ● ▮

Moyra paced the small space of the underground room. Driskoll sat on the floor and leaned against a wall, watching her.

The single candle burned in its holder, which they'd placed in the middle of the floor. The candlelight threw eerie shadows across the dirt walls of the pit. The shadows loomed and danced as the candle flickered, making Driskoll think of ghosts and other strange things that lurked in dark corners.

Driskoll wasn't sure, but he didn't think much time had passed since they'd heard the door shut and they knew they were trapped.

In a hole.

In Lexos's home.

If the situation weren't so serious, Driskoll might have laughed at how absurd it all was.

"And to think that just a few days ago, I was complaining how bored I was," Driskoll said.

"You find this exciting?" Moyra shot back.

"If you mean sitting in a hole in the ground, no, this is not exciting. But I know that you'll figure some way out of here."

Moyra snorted. "Like what! We've already tried everything!"

They'd stood on the wooden ladder that led into the pit, and had tried to raise the trapdoor. But the bolt was too strong. They'd considered burning the door with the candle, but then they'd realized that the ceiling, including the door, was covered by a sheet of iron. Dig their way out? They'd scratched for a few moments, only to find that the dirt was more clay than loose soil. All they'd gotten for their efforts was tons of dirt under their fingernails and muddy knees.

"If only I had my tools!" Moyra absently traced a circle on the dirt floor with her foot.

"If I had my sword, we could chop our way out," Driskoll added.

"Well, you don't have your sword and I don't have my tools," Moyra said. She screeched in frustration. "You know, I don't even care what Lexos does with us when he comes back. I only care about what's happening right now. And the fact that I don't know is driving me nuts!" She glared up at the trapdoor and shook her fist. "H-h-holy potatoes! I hate this!"

Driskoll threw up his hands. "What is it with you and the holy potatoes?"

Moyra looked sheepish. "My mom told me I shouldn't curse so much, and that's—" She stopped and cocked her ear toward the door "Did you hear that?"

Driskoll shook his head. "I didn't hear anything.

Moyra held up a hand. "Shh! There! There it is again!"

Driskoll stretched his legs and stood. He heard it, too. "That scratching noise? It's probably just a mouse or something."

"Great," Moyra said. "Just great. Now we have rats to keep us company."

"I said mouse, not rat."

Moyra rolled her eyes. "Oh, that makes me feel so much better." She walked up the ladder and waited.

"What are you doing now?"

"Shh!" She held her fist below the door, waiting, waiting—then she pounded as loudly as she could.

"What did you do that for?" Driskoll asked, peering up at her.

"To scare away the rat, of course."

"Rat?" said a voice on the other side of the door. "I beg your pardon. I may be small, but I am no rat!"

CHAPTER

12

Moyra was so surprised, she nearly fell off the ladder. She climbed down quickly and stood next to Driskoll. They both peered at the door above them.

"Hello? Are you still down there?" the voice spoke again.

"We weren't imagining it," Driskoll whispered. "There really *is* someone there."

"Well, let's not stand around with our mouths open," Moyra said. "Yes!" she shouted. "We're here! Below the door!"

"Why, you are, aren't you?" the voice said.

Driskoll didn't stop to think who the voice belonged to. The voice meant freedom. The voice meant escape. "Can you lift the door?" he hollered up. "I think it might be heavy!"

"Heavy, you say?" They heard a few scurries, then a squeaky noise, like metal rubbing against metal. "Bit of a bolt, you see," the voice said. "Now, let's see if this door is, indeed, heavy."

Driskoll watched, astonished, as the door inched its way upward.

"A little help would be nice," the voice said.

Both Driskoll and Moyra fought for position on the ladder. They both thrust their hands against the door, and with the aid of their mysterious helper, the door flew back effortlessly. Moyra bounded up the ladder first, with Driskoll a close second. They didn't give a moment's thought to the candle still burning on the dirt floor.

Scanning the room, Moyra wrinkled her forehead. "I don't see anyone."

"He must be here somewhere." Driskoll looked quickly around the room. The trapdoor he and Moyra had flung upward now lay open on the floor, revealing the pit below. Mystified, he called out. "Hello? Rat-person? Where are you?"

"The door that you thought might be heavy? Well, it is rather heavy when it is lying across one's person."

"Oh, my goodness!" Moyra exclaimed, pointing at the trapdoor. Beneath the slab of wood, Driskoll saw two wiggling feet. Driskoll ran around to the other side of the pit, hoisted up the door, and let it drop shut with a thud.

"Thank you so much!" Driskoll said. "We have something urgent we have to do, and . . . " Driskoll's words trailed off. He watched as the most grotesque being he'd ever seen wobbled to his feet, then began brushing himself off.

The creature looked a bit like a dwarf, but not quite as big or as broad. His tall, rounded ears stuck out from the sides of his head, and his queer nose hung, long and bulbous. He wore short trousers that revealed hairy legs, and boots that were ankle-high and had pointy toes. A loose tunic with a wide belt completed his attire.

Momentarily startled, Moyra managed to ask, "And who do we have the pleasure of thanking?"

"Pleased to meet you, too." The grotesque creature smiled and his face crinkled, like a piece of old parchment. "I am Gryphyll!"

Moyra bowed. "I'm Moyra, and this is Driskoll."

"A treasure! A treasure!" said the little fellow.

"Don't you mean 'pleasure'?" Driskoll said, shaking his hand. The chubby little fingers wrapped around two of Driskoll's own. Driskoll expected the hand to feel moist and slimy, like that of a toad or a fish. Instead, the little fingers were quite strong.

"Nope, treasure, treasure it is!" The face crinkled even more.

Driskoll looked about Lexos's hut. It suddenly dawned on him that anyone with a connection to Lexos should probably not be trusted, even if he had saved their lives. "Um, I don't mean to be rude or ungrateful, but what are you doing here?"

"Why, I live here!" Gryphyll said.

"You live here?" Moyra asked. "I thought Lexos lived here."

"Yes, Lexos. Not a very nice man, is he? Seemed to think the hut was empty, and just walked right in." The little creature hobbled away from the door and across the room. "Never bothered to look around, he didn't, and only lit a few candles. It's very easy for me to hide in the shadows, don't you know."

Driskoll nodded. "We can see that." He studied the fellow closely. "What are you, Gryphyll? Half dwarf?"

"What am I?" the creature asked, perplexed. "Why, I'm Gryphyll!"

"Yes, but you see . . ." Driskoll pointed to himself. "I'm a human. It's not who I am, it's what I am."

The creature shook his head. "I'm Gryphyll, that's all I know."

"Whatever," Driskoll said abruptly. "This has been really fun, but we must be going. We have important matters to see to."

"Yes, nasty business, that. I heard your conversation with Lexos. He has your mother, has he?"

"In a way," Moyra said. As she spoke, she re-bolted the door and kicked dirt across it so Lexos wouldn't realize right away that they had escaped. "It's a long story."

"Something about a medallion, too, if I heard right."

"Yes, you heard right." Driskoll spied their gear in the corner where Lexos had tossed it. He handed Moyra her things, then buckled his sword back around his waist. "Look, whatever you are, we hate to be rescued and run, but we really have to go," Driskoll said. "We have to find my brother and Lexos and make sure Moyra's mother is all right."

"I completely understand," said the accommodating little fellow. He stood there with his hands folded in front of him, his small purple eyes twinkling up at Moyra.

A silly smile came over Moyra's face. "Driskoll, I think we should take him with us."

Gryphyll beamed.

"What!" Driskoll shook his head. "No! Absolutely not."

"We can't leave him here," she insisted. "Who knows what Lexos will do to him after he discovers we're gone."

"Moyra, we don't even know who he is or what he is. He could be working for Lexos for all we know."

Moyra waved that away. "Doubtful." She turned to Gryphyll. "Look, we have to move quickly, but do you want to come with us?"

Gryphyll smile grew brighter, revealing a few teeth, and a few spaces where teeth might once have been. "Quite kind of you, miss!" He looked up at Driskoll. "But does the young sir wish my company too?"

Driskoll rolled his eyes and glanced at Moyra. "Oh, all right. I don't exactly like this, but I know you. You won't let it rest, and we'll spend the next ten minutes arguing about it." Driskoll turned to Gryphyll. "Come on then. We have to hurry."

Gryphyll waddled over and took both Moyra and Driskoll's hands, smiling all the while. He looked as if he wanted to swing between them, like a child on a sunny afternoon at the park. "Don't worry, sir. I'm swifter on my feet than you'd believe."

"I hope so," Driskoll said. "Because suddenly I feel like we're running out of time."

CHAPTER

13

For the first time that he could ever remember, Driskoll found himself afraid to enter Watchers' Hall.

It felt strange, like now he was the criminal and had something to hide.

But it wasn't so much that they had something to hide, but that they were trying to hide from Lexos.

They stood in the shadow of the building: he, Moyra, and their new friend, Gryphyll.

"We can't just go strolling in," Driskoll said. "If Lexos is in there talking to Dad, he'll see us and will know we've escaped."

"So true, so true!" Gryphyll chirped.

Driskoll glanced at the little thing briefly, then back up at the door to the hall.

"They've had plenty of time to talk to your dad," Moyra said.

"They could be freeing your mom right now," Driskoll said.

Moyra moved from foot to foot. "Well, I can't just stand here. Come on!"

Before Driskoll could stop her, Moyra ran through the doors of Watchers' Hall. Gryphyll tugged on Driskoll's hand, pulling Driskoll along. Driskoll groaned, knowing he had no choice. He had to go after her.

"You're pretty strong for a little guy," Driskoll said, looking down at Gryphyll. Gryphyll grunted and tried to yank Driskoll through the door.

"Wait!" Driskoll whispered. "We need to make sure we don't see Lexos."

"So right!" said Gryphyll.

Driskoll opened the door a crack and peered through. He didn't see anyone he knew, or anyone who might know him. Not even Moyra. Holding a finger to his lips, Driskoll eased the door open and crept inside. Taking his cue from Gryphyll, he clung to the shadows. Only after they'd passed Guffy's desk, unseen, did Driskoll let out a breath.

A rock hit him on the shoulder.

Driskoll glanced in the direction that the rock had come, seeing only a dark, shadowy stairwell. "What the—"

"Shh!"

"Moyra!"

Driskoll ducked into the dark stairwell, pulling Gryphyll in behind him. Moyra crouched there in the dim light.

"Good choice," Driskoll whispered, squatting beside her. "My dad's office isn't far from here. That's probably where Lexos and Kellach are."

Moyra didn't answer. She was intently scanning the hallway, listening.

"Moyra?" Driskoll asked softly. "What do you think?"

"I think—I think our timing is perfect!" she said.

Driskoll saw Moyra reach into her pocket. She pulled out another small stone. Then, before he could stop her, he saw her throw it into the hallway.

"Moyra! What are you—"

"Ouch!" came a voice from the hall.

Kellach came into the doorway.

His mouth fell open and his eyes grew wide.

"Don't stand there like a fish," Moyra said. "Get over here!"

Kellach glanced over each shoulder, then joined them in the stairwell. Driskoll turned and walked down a few steps so they could all hide together.

"What happened?" Kellach said. "How did you get out?"

Moyra put her arm around their new friend. "Kellach, I'd like you to meet Gryphyll."

Kellach's eyes got bigger, but he reached out a hand to shake the one Gryphyll offered. "A treasure, a treasure!" said Gryphyll.

"Uh, don't you mean pleasure?" Kellach said.

Driskoll shook his head. "Don't bother. It's not worth it."

"I still don't understand," Kellach said.

"We'll explain later," Moyra said. She grabbed his arm. "What happened? Is my mom free? Did Lexos try anything? What did your dad—"

Kellach held up a hand and laughed. "Everything's fine. And yes, Lexos was a bit of a creep. He kept prophesizing doom to all of us, blah, blah, blah." He laughed again. "You know, he actually sounded pretty stupid on a bright sunny day, like today. I couldn't take anything he said seriously."

"What did you do?" Driskoll asked.

"I kept walking. Fast. I let him ramble on. I could tell he wanted to grab the medallion and run. He kept staring at the pouch, and a few times I even caught him reaching out his hand. But I held on tight. And I told him how much better it would look for his reputation if he saved an innocent woman from the prison." Kellach paused, then shook his head. "Of course, I don't think he really cares about that. But he did it."

"Where is he now?" Driskoll said.

"He's on his way home. He left a little bit before I did."

"We could have run into him!" Driskoll said.

"But we didn't," said Moyra. "So what now?"

Kellach smiled. "Well, now we go see your mom!"

Moyra's face lit up. "Really? She's free?"

"Of course!" Kellach said. "It all went exactly as I had planned. Lexos told Dad he had made a mistake. He asked him to drop the charges."

Driskoll felt heat flush through his chest. "Dad! I forgot about Dad! How did he take all of this?"

Kellach's smile wavered. "Not well. Not only was he shocked to see me walk through the door with Lexos, but he was even more surprised when I took the medallion from my robes."

"I bet," said Driskoll, his stomach going all queasy.

"Yeah. His face turned a nice shade of red when I told him what we'd done."

"Think we'll get in trouble?"

"Probably." Kellach stood up straighter. "But it doesn't matter. The medallion is safe, Moyra's mom is free, and Lexos is none the wiser."

"Hurray! Hurray!" said Gryphyll. "A treasure, a treasure!"

Kellach looked at the queer little troll. "Who is this guy again?"

"I'll explain everything," said Moyra. "But let's get my mom first."

She was already ahead of them, up the stairs, and through the door. Now that they knew Lexos was no longer in the building, they had nothing to fear. They ran down the hallway, waved to a few surprised watchers, and practically flew into the foyer. Gryphyll giggled and waggled along with them, as if it were all a big game.

The door leading to the prison cells stood open, and Royma shivered beside the duty desk, as Guffy filled out the last of the paperwork.

Moyra bolted past Guffy and didn't stop until she had wrapped her arms around her mother's waist. Driskoll and Kellach stopped just inside the door.

"I knew you'd think of something, my clever girl." Royma brushed a ragged strand of red hair from Moyra's cheek.

"Oh, Mom!" Moyra cried, leaning her head on her mother's shoulder. "I wish none of this had ever happened."

"It's not something I'll soon be forgetting, that's for sure," Royma said.

Driskoll felt a lump rise in his throat, and he thought he saw Kellach wipe a tear from his eye.

Gryphyll openly showed his emotions and blubbered all over himself.

"So, you see, even though we disobeyed you,"—Kellach cleared his throat uneasily— "everything worked out in the end."

Driskoll and Kellach sat on one side of Zendric's long table. Zendric sat on the other. Moyra had taken Gryphyll home with her so she could spend some time with her mom.

The two boys had to face Zendric alone.

The old wizard kept his hands folded in front of him, the sleeves of his robes making wings on the tabletop. His face had no expression as he listened to Kellach and Driskoll explain what had happened. In fact, Zendric barely moved at all.

Driskoll rubbed his hands against his thighs and felt a trickle of sweat roll down his back. The room wasn't warm, but Driskoll felt like it was a hundred degrees.

He and Kellach waited breathlessly for Zendric to speak. A log fell in the fireplace. Somewhere outside a bird whistled.

The wizard unfolded his hands and placed them palm-down on the table. He pushed himself up with great effort. Driskoll and Kellach watched as the wizard walked to the fireplace and stared into the flames. He placed his hands behind his back, and bowed his head.

Finally the wizard turned around. The fire lit him from behind, casting his face in shadows. Only his eyes shimmered bright.

"I want to be angry, with all of you," Zendric began.

Driskoll ran his hands over his thighs again. Could Zendric be letting them off? Could they really not be in trouble for sneaking out and facing Lexos alone? Could they—

"But I fear you have a much greater task in front of you, and my anger would not help at a time like this."

"A-a greater task?" Driskoll said.

"Yes, my friends, a greater task." Zendric paused and looked into each of their eyes. "For now the true test has come."

"True test?" Kellach asked. "What do you mean?"

Zendric folded his hands on the table. "Do you remember what I said we must do with the medallion, once we had it?"

"You told us it had to be returned to the silver dragon who made it," Kellach said.

Zendric leaned forward. "The time has come for you to do so."

"But how hard could that be?" Driskoll said. "It can't be as hard as facing down Lexos."

"That's right," Kellach said. "And this time, we'll have you along to help us. We'll help each other."

Zendric shook his head. "I cannot go with you, lads."

Driskoll saw Kellach's body go rigid. "You're not sick, are you?" Kellach asked.

Zendric chuckled. "No, lad."

"Then I don't understand," said Kellach.

Zendric reached across the table with both hands and grasped one of Kellach's and one of Driskoll's. Driskoll sat back, surprised by the wizard's touch. His heart began to beat faster, and he was suddenly afraid of what Zendric was going to say next.

"The medallion's appearance was not a random event, my boy. It was a sign that the time for your quest has come."

"What quest?" Driskoll asked.

"At some point in their lives, every Knight in our order must journey to find a silver dragon. Then that dragon becomes the Knight's ally for all time."

"I still don't understand why you can't come," Kellach said.

"Finding the dragon cannot be done with a seasoned wizard or an experienced knight along for help." Zendric leaned closer. "You must prove yourself on this quest, and if you do so, then you will be full-fledged members of our ancient order."

"And if we don't?" Driskoll asked.

Zendric released their hands and sat back. "Then that's as it should be."

Kellach grasped the edge of the table. "What does that mean?"

Zendric folded his hands again. "Kellach, being a Knight of the Silver Dragon is a great honor."

"Of course it is! We've never—"

Zendric held up a hand. "To become a true Knight takes more than just a ceremony and a silver pin."

Driskoll gripped the hilt of his sword. "So, what you're saying is, that if we don't find the silver dragon, we're not going to be Knights?"

Zendric nodded once. "It was not meant to be."

"Gods!" Driskoll gasped.

Zendric smiled. "Yes, Driskoll. The task before you is immense, in more ways than one. Lexos must never get his hand on the medallion, and you, my friends, must complete this quest on your own to find out if you are truly worthy of being named Knights of the Silver Dragon."

Kellach stood suddenly, his chair flinging over, his blond hair flying around his shoulders. He stared up at his mentor.

Driskoll thought he looked very wizard-like.

"We can do it," Kellach said.

"It will not be easy," Zendric began.

Driskoll muttered under his breath, "And that should be a surprise?"

Kellach shot him a look.

"The journey will prove treacherous, I'm afraid," Zendric continued. "The silver dragons have hidden themselves for many years now. You will have a difficult time finding one in these troubled times."

"What do you suggest we do?" Kellach asked.

Zendric stood and walked across the room. Going to an over-stuffed bookshelf, he lifted one of the books. Driskoll craned his neck to see around the wizard, and he saw a stone slide out of the wall. Zendric reached his hand inside, brought it out, replaced the stone, and came back to the table.

"First of all, do not let the medallion out of your sight." He opened his palm, and the real medallion lay there, glowing with a soft silver light.

Driskoll looked away before it could affect him.

"Not a problem," Kellach said. "I'll keep it in here, next to me at all times." He showed Zendric a leather pouch he wore around his waist and under his robes.

Zendric closed his palm over the medallion, and Driskoll looked up again. "Good. Also, never use the medallion."

"But what if we must?" Kellach asked.

"Silver dragons created the medallion for their use only," said Zendric. "When it is used by creatures other than silver dragons, its powers begin to change and adapt to the true nature of the owner."

"So, in the hands of Lexos, the medallion could become evil?" Kellach said.

"That's correct. I don't know how the medallion might change if you, Kellach, or I were to use it to extremes. We never know what might be revealed about our natures when magic is involved. Because my powers are so much stronger than yours, it is not wise for me to handle it any longer."

With his palm still closed, Zendric reached across the table. Driskoll saw the medallion drop into Kellach's hand, then Kellach swiftly placed it in the pouch and secured the top with a toggle.

"So how do we go about finding a silver dragon?" he asked.

CHAPTER

14

"I guess Dad was glad to hear we'd be staying at Zendric's for a while," Driskoll said, hoisting the pack on his back.

"Yeah," said Kellach. "I almost feel bad. He seemed really tired of the whole thing."

"Or maybe he was just tired of us," Driskoll suggested.

Moyra blew a stray strand of red hair from her eyes. "At least he didn't punish you like you thought he would."

"That's what's so weird about it," said Kellach. "I expected to hear we were grounded forever and that we could never go to Zendric's again. Instead, he seemed relieved to see us go."

"Well, we'll try to be better, once this quest is over, right, Kellach?"

Kellach twisted his face. "Yeah, right."

"Do you really think we'll find a dragon?" Moyra asked.

"Of course we will," Driskoll said. "Won't we, Kellach?"

Driskoll could tell his older brother mulled the question over in his mind. Driskoll wouldn't have expected anything less from him. When Kellach finally spoke, his words were a bit like something Zendric would say. "I believe that if we're meant to find the silver dragon, then it will be."

"Ooo!" Moyra mocked. "Listen to you! So mysterious and worldly!"

"He is, isn't he?" Driskoll said, laughing. "You need to lighten up a bit, Kell. Look! It's a beautiful day, and the entire realm is stretched out before us!"

Driskoll waved his arm, taking in the view that surrounded them. After walking for about an hour, they stood on a slight hill that offered a stunning view. Curston lay behind them, its walls wrapping around the protrusion of dwellings and shops that formed the town. The tall spire of St. Cuthbert's, the tallest building in Curston, rose sharply from the town center. Driskoll even thought he could see Zendric's tower off to one side, but he couldn't be sure.

Moving away from Curston, the scenery spread out in glorious patches of fields and meadows. Ever so gently, the land began to rise, and as Driskoll turned back, he noticed the jagged peaks of the mountains that rose in the distance, the sun glinting off the snow that capped their peaks.

Raising a hand to shield his eyes, Driskoll pointed to the mountains. "I suppose that's where we're headed?"

Kellach nodded. "Zendric says silver dragons are known to live in those mountains. He drew a map, but with peaks as obvious as those, I don't think we'll get lost. He did say it would take several days, though. And that it would be dangerous."

"Dangerous?" Driskoll asked, willing his voice not to shake. "What kind of dangerous? Like goblin dangerous?"

Kellach nodded. "Zendric said there's a goblin this big"—he lifted his hand high above his head—"and he's been looking for you ever since our last trip to the ruins."

Driskoll's eyes went wide. "Really?"

Moyra glared at Kellach and put her arm over Driskoll's shoulder. "Just ignore him, Driskoll. He's teasing you. You know goblins only live in the ruins and we're nowhere near there."

"Besides," Kellach hoisted up his pack. "With me in charge of this expedition, you two have nothing to fear. With all the spells I know now, I can protect you from whatever danger might come our way."

Driskoll scoffed. "Right. Just like you always do."

Driskoll and Moyra looked at each other and tried not to laugh, but Kellach was being so mature and, well, wizardly, that they couldn't help it. Driskoll had to watch his balance. He laughed so hard he almost toppled over from the weight of his pack.

"You two think this is funny?" Kellach asked.

Moyra wiped away a tear. "No, Kell. We think *you're* funny."

It took a moment, but Kellach's face slowly burst into a grin. "Yeah, I guess I was being a bit much."

"That's okay, Kell," Driskoll said, straightening and repositioning his pack. "We won't hold it against you."

"Gee, I'm all mushed up," Kellach said.

The threesome trekked across the countryside and into the forest. Kellach had brought along Locky, his familiar, a mechanical dragon. Every once in a while, the little dragon showed itself, peeking out from the top of Kellach's pack.

All in all, the hours passed pleasantly. It was so pleasant that Driskoll almost forgot that they were on a quest to find an ancient beast with mythical powers.

A branch snapped behind him.

Driskoll stopped, and Moyra stumbled into him.

"Hey!"

"Did you hear that?" Driskoll asked.

"Hear what?"

Driskoll listened, but he didn't hear another sound. Still, he had the distinct feeling that someone was following them. Or watching them.

"Hey, Kell!" he called softly to his brother. "Do you, um, you know, sense anything?"

"I sense that you're a pain in the—"

"No, really. I don't know why, but I have this feeling that someone is following us."

Kellach and Moyra paused and listened.

"I don't hear anything," Kellach said finally.

"I swear I heard something, like a twig breaking."

"It was probably just the wind, or maybe even one of us who stepped on something."

"Maybe," Driskoll said. But he didn't believe it. The feeling didn't go away, and as they walked deeper and deeper into the forest, his apprehension grew. The sun shone directly overhead, and Driskoll knew they'd soon stop for food. His stomach rumbled, and he thought about the cheese and apples in their packs. And honey cakes and—

He heard it again! Another sound this time, like something had fallen. A soft thump in the forest.

Driskoll looked quickly behind him, his hand poised on the hilt of his sword. He still didn't see a thing. The forest appeared empty except for the trees, the leaves, and an occasional squirrel darting by.

Turning back, Driskoll was about to forget about it, when a movement caught his eye.

Maybe he'd been hearing things, but Driskoll knew his eyes weren't playing tricks on him.

"Moyra! Kellach! Hold up!" Driskoll hissed. "Something *is* out there. This time I saw it."

Kellach and Moyra turned and tossed him a "what now?" look.

"Driskoll, we have a lot of ground to cover," said Kellach. "We don't have time for this."

"I swear, Kell, this time I didn't just hear something, I saw something too."

"Well, where is that something now?" Moyra asked, hands on hips.

"I-I don't know," Driskoll said, confused.

"Maybe we should look around anyway, Kell," Moyra suggested. "If Driskoll is hearing and seeing things, we don't want to be surprised if something really is out there."

Kellach sighed, but agreed. "All right. Let's spread out a bit and see if we find anything."

Relieved that they finally believed him, Driskoll looked behind trees and kicked up piles of leaves. He came to a large boulder and another movement caught his eye.

"Over here! It's over here!"

Driskoll dashed behind the boulder, just in time to see a pair of stubby legs disappear into the hollow of a tree. He ran after it, lifted his sword from its sheath, and said, "I order you to come out and show yourself, whatever you may be!"

CHAPTER

15

A grotesque—and very familiar—head poked out from the tree.

"Gryphyll!" Driskoll bent down to help the little troll up. "What are you doing here?"

"Why, I'm following you," he said cheerfully.

"What do you mean, you're following us?" Driskoll asked

Gryphyll dusted himself off and explained. "Well, I couldn't help overhearing your plans when you explained them to Moyra. I thought, how exciting! Much more exciting than my life back in Curston. So here I am!"

Moyra and Kellach ran up when they saw Gryphyll.

"Look what I found," Driskoll announced, resheathing his sword.

"Gryphyll, you were supposed to remain with Zendric," Moyra scolded.

Gryphyll looked slightly guilty, but only for a moment. "Yes, well, Zendric seemed like a very busy man, and I didn't want to get in his way."

"So you decided to get in our way instead," Kellach said.

The little man's face fell, several layers of wrinkled skin dipping below his chin. "Get in your way? But I can be extremely helpful." The wrinkles lifted again into a smile. "Yes! Yes, I can!"

"Helpful?" Kellach asked doubtfully. "How?"

"Well, I know which berries are right for eating!"

"That's an admirable skill," Moyra agreed.

"And I can tie any kind of rope that needs tying! If we have to climb mountains, my knots will never break!"

"Also worthwhile," Moyra said. She put her arm around the little creature's shoulder and smiled down warmly at him. "I think you'll find that there are a lot of things Gryphyll can do."

Driskoll help up his hand. "Hang on a second here. Do we really know who Gryphyll is?"

"He's a resident of Curston," Moyra said. "You know, living at the hut on the edge of town."

"Until that nasty Lexos showed up," Gryphyll said. He scrunched up his face as if he'd bitten into something sour.

"Right," Driskoll said. "He lived in Lexos's hut."

Moyra placed her hands on her hips. "Driskoll, what is your point?"

"My point is that we really don't know anything about him."

"I know that he saved our lives!" she shot back.

"Yes, but where, exactly, did he come from?"

"He told us—he'd been living in Lexos's hut—"

"Exactly!" Driskoll shouted over her. "I mean, don't you think it's strange that until yesterday we didn't know who Gryphyll was? Then he just happens to be in Lexos's hut, where he rescues Moyra and me, and now he just happens to show up here, offering to help us return the medallion to the silver dragon?"

"Go on," said Kellach.

"Well, what if . . . what if our newest and best-est friend Gryphyll here is really a spy, and he's working for Lexos!"

"A spy?" Moyra burst out laughing. "You've really lost it this time. Look at him!" Driskoll looked at the beaming, silly creature. "Does that look like a spy to you?"

"How do we know he's *not* a spy?" Driskoll persisted. "Think about it! He knows all our plans from being at Zendric's. What if he's really reporting back to Lexos somehow? Like, maybe he's Lexos's familiar, like Locky is your familiar, Kell? After all, he showed up the same time Lexos did."

At that moment, Kellach's familiar appeared, peeking over the edge of Kellach's pack. Locky gawked when it saw Gryphyll and flapped its wings.

Gryphyll spied the creature and shouted with delight.

Locky gawked louder and flew up to rest on Kellach's shoulder.

"Look-ee! A silver bird!" Gryphyll waddled over and gazed up at Locky. He clapped and pointed, his wrinkles waggling on his face. "It can fly! Look-ee! It can fly!"

Moyra pointed to Gryphyll. "Are you serious, Driskoll? You think *that* is a spy? Look at him!"

Gryphyll tried to reach for the mechanical dragon, but instead tripped and stumbled forward. Kellach reached out a hand to steady him.

"It could be an act," Driskoll warned.

"Could be," Kellach said, smiling down at Gryphyll, "but not likely. I think he's just what he says he is."

"And what's that?" Driskoll asked.

"He's a little lost soul, looking for a home," Moyra said, her voice full of feeling.

Driskoll rolled his eyes. He could see that Moyra had grown attached to the troll, or whatever he was.

Kellach looked up at the sun. "I don't know about you two, but I'm starving. I think we're due for a break about now anyway. Want to rest here for a bit and eat some lunch?"

As if on cue, Gryphyll's stomach growled loudly. He rubbed his belly and smiled.

"I take that as a yes," Moyra said. She leaped up onto a boulder, unstrapped the pack from her back, and sat down. "And I think this is the perfect spot."

Kellach hopped up on the rock, and Driskoll joined him, a bit more slowly. He still wasn't convinced that Gryphyll was just a silly little toad. He wasn't convinced that Gryphyll was a spy either. But just what Gryphyll was, Driskoll couldn't figure out.

Gryphyll scrambled up onto the boulder and plopped down in front of Driskoll, Moyra, and Kellach.

"Let me guess," Driskoll said. "You didn't bring any food."

Gryphyll lifted his shoulders and held out his hands. "So sorry, so sorry to be a burden. A burden, I am. But I'll make up for it, you'll see!"

"It's fine, Gryphyll," Moyra said. She reached into her pack, rummaged around, and produced a pear. "Here. Would you like one of these?"

"A treasure, a treasure!" Gryphyll said, snatching the fruit from her palm. He giggled as he bit into it, squirting pear juice out the sides of his mouth.

"Hmph. Some spy." Moyra gave Driskoll a sidelong glare. Then she settled back to eat some cheese with a hunk of bread.

Driskoll kept one eye on Gryphyll as he rummaged through his own pack. He pulled out an apple and bit into it, lifting his face to the sun shining through the trees. The forest was lush and cool, overgrown with ferns and bushes and leafy boughs.

A tall oak grew to one side of the boulder, and opposite the boulder loomed a steep cliff wall. The narrow trail on which they'd been walking wove its way between the boulder and the cliff. With the boulder on one side and the cliff on the other, their lunch spot was secluded and protected. No monster could creep up on them without them seeing it first.

A large pocket of sunshine fell on the boulder, warming it. Driskoll inhaled the fresh scent of moss and leaves, and a light breeze lifted the hair off his forehead. The sunshine lulled Driskoll into a daydream, and he closed his eyes, the pleasant thoughts of practicing his swordplay with a seasoned knight filling his mind.

A whirring sound swiftly brought him back to the forest. Driskoll opened his eyes in time to see Kellach's mechanical dragon whizzing past them.

Gryphyll began to chase Locky across the boulder. He reached out to catch him, but instead caught nothing but air. Gryphyll chortled as he fell off the rock.

"Gryphyll!" Moyra cried. She crawled toward the edge of the boulder and kneeled next to Driskoll.

Driskoll peered over the edge. Gryphyll lay below in a soft pile of leaves, laughing uncontrollably.

"He certainly is goofy," Driskoll admitted.

"Yeah, some spy." Kellach laughed.

"Hey, you never know. It doesn't hurt to be cautious." Driskoll tossed the apple core into a nearby thicket and began tying the top of his pack.

Driskoll stopped.

This time he didn't hear something or see something. This time he felt something.

The boulder shuddered beneath him.

Driskoll reached out a hand to steady himself. He placed his hand on the boulder, and he could feel tingly vibrations on his skin. He looked at his pack and saw that the strings that dangled from the top trembled, then jumped up and down, as if someone were bouncing the pack on his or her knee.

The boulder shuddered again, this time with a slight moan, as if someone were stretching and yawning and trying to wake up.

Driskoll glanced at Kellach and Moyra. Moyra had her hands braced on either side of her, gripping the hard rock so she wouldn't slide off. Kellach frantically snatched at his apple, trying to gather up the fruit before it rolled off the boulder.

"What's happening?" Driskoll called out.

"I'm not sure," Kellach said, scrambling after the rolling apple.

Suddenly the boulder shifted violently and thrust upward. With nothing to hold on to, Driskoll felt himself pushed into the air. He covered his head, certain he was about to crash into a branch from the oak tree. But gravity took over and pulled him back down, down into a pile of leaves between the boulder and the cliff wall. The leaves were soft, and Driskoll didn't feel bruised as much as confused. He staggered to his feet, brushing leaves from his hair and eyes, and made sure that no bones were broken.

Kellach was still sitting on the ground, his legs spread out before him, his arms holding his body up from behind. Moyra hopped on one leg, like she was trying to clear water from her ear.

Gryphyll rolled over toward Driskoll like a fallen log, his little gray head bobbing up and down as he came closer, and Locky flapped his silver wings and landed beside Kellach.

"What happened?" Moyra asked in between hops.

Driskoll looked at the boulder that they'd been sitting on, but he didn't recognize it. No longer was it a smooth sunny spot to have lunch. No. Somehow, the boulder had sprouted stubby legs, chubby arms, and a block-shaped head. A hole opened on the blockhead, right where someone's mouth might be, and two pebbled eyes, like knobs of coal, glittered darkly.

"I don't think the question is 'what happened,'" Driskoll said, pointing at the stone creature, "but 'what is that?'"

CHAPTER

16

Kellach stood slowly, his gaze glued to the boulder. "It's a galeb duhr," he said. "Stupid of me to have forgotten that they blend into the forest by resembling rocks."

Moyra, Kellach, and Driskoll backed up slowly, Driskoll unsheathing his sword. The galeb duhr rose above them, about half the height of the oak tree to the left. It inched forward, one stubby foot claiming ground, dragging its boulder body with it.

"It's not moving very fast," Driskoll said. "Maybe we can outrun it."

"Good idea," said Moyra, "but where are we going to run?" She pointed behind her, and Driskoll saw what she meant. They were trapped. The wall of the cliff that Driskoll had admired while eating lunch now pressed up against their backs.

"Could we climb the wall, do you think?" Driskoll asked, scanning the height above him.

"With what?" Moyra asked. "Our stuff is scattered all over the place."

She waved a hand, and Driskoll saw their gear strewn about the path. He spied a rope, tangled in the leaves, but it was closer to the tree than to the cliff.

Driskoll turned his attention back to the galeb duhr. The monster made slow, steady progress toward them, one slow shuffling step at a time. Its dark cavernous mouth remained opened, as if in a silent moan, and its dark eyes glared from round sockets, topped by eyebrow-like rocky ledges.

"What are we going to do?" Moyra said as the monster stomped closer.

"Kell," Driskoll turned to his brother. "Maybe a levitation spell or something could get us out of here?"

"I can only move two people at a time," Kellach reminded them. Locky chirped excitedly on his shoulder.

"That might be okay," Driskoll said. "He's not moving very fast."

Just then, Moyra saw Gryphyll roll through the leaves, right in front of the galeb duhr.

"Gryphyll!" she cried.

The galeb duhr raised its thick stubby leg.

Moyra rushed over and reached under the monster. The leg started to lower.

"Watch out!" Driskoll shouted.

Moyra scooped up Gryphyll and ran back to the cliff. She didn't look back, but Driskoll saw the galeb duhr's large, boulder leg crush down on the spot where Gryphyll and Moyra had been only two seconds before.

Moyra placed Gryphyll gently on the ground.

"It looks like you've now saved *my* life," Gryphyll said, his voice a bit shaken. "That creature doesn't have very nice manners, does he? Throwing you off just as we were finishing up our lunch."

"I think we're about to *be* lunch," Driskoll said.

"Hmph! Monsters!" Gryphyll snorted.

The galeb duhr crept ever closer, its mouth now open in a hungry roar. The ground beneath their feet shook, causing Driskoll to lose his balance. He thrust his sword into the ground to steady himself.

Moyra grabbed the rock wall behind her so she wouldn't fall. "Kellach! Do something!" she shouted.

"Like what?" he shouted back.

"Cast something!" Moyra called. "Anything! Maybe the magic will distract it like it did with the ormyrr."

Kellach shrugged. "Worth a try."

He raised his arms and summoned up a burst of air. The dry, brown leaves on the forest floor swirled and spun. A few acorns joined the mix, and pretty soon a fantastic twirling performance filled the space between them and the galeb duhr.

The galeb duhr lifted another stubby leg. Its uplifted leg crashed to the ground, sending tremors across the earth. Driskoll, Kellach, Gryphyll, and Moyra braced themselves against the cliff wall, but they still wobbled and clutched at each other to stay upright.

"What now?" Moyra asked.

"I-I'm not sure," Kellach said. "Driskoll?"

Driskoll looked at Moyra and Kellach, then he faced the galeb duhr. He gripped the hilt of his sword with both hands and slowly raised the sword above his head. The galeb duhr was nearly upon them. One more booming step, and the monster would be in reach of his sword.

Driskoll held tighter to the hilt. "I don't know what will happen when I strike, but I think it's our last chance."

"Go for it!" Moyra shouted.

The galeb duhr lifted its leg, ready to take one more step. It bent its boulder body closer to Driskoll, Kellach, and Moyra. Locky let out a screech and dived inside Kellach's robes.

Steady, Driskoll said to himself. He stared up into the dark, glittering eyes of the monster, then took a look into the dark cave-like mouth. He didn't see any teeth, just a chasm that looked like it could swallow a person whole.

Steady, Driskoll said to himself again. He regripped his sword and waited for the galeb duhr to lower its leg. Then I'll smash my sword on one of its arms, he thought, and we'll see what—

The galeb duhr roared, a deep, thunderous sound. Pebbles fell from the cliff behind them and rained down upon their head. Branches quivered on the oak tree, and Driskoll felt his sword vibrate. A burst of hot wind lashed their faces and blew their hair back.

"That's it!" Driskoll shouted. "I have had enough of you!" He channeled all his energy into his arms, and swung the sword as hard as he could.

CHAPTER

17

Kellach grabbed Driskoll's arm.

"What are you doing?" Driskoll yelled.

"Shh!" Kellach said. "Listen!"

At first, Driskoll heard nothing but the rumbling of the earth and the heavy breathing of the galeb duhr, its hot breath heating his face. Then, beneath the rumbling, another sound emerged. A soft sound. A . . . a humming sound?

Gryphyll was humming.

"What are you doing?" Driskoll turned to Gryphyll, who sat against the wall, in between Kellach and Moyra. "This isn't the time to sing!"

"I always hum when I'm nervous," Gryphyll hummed. "Try it, Driskoll. You'll find it's quite pleasant."

"You're kidding, right?"

"Maybe he's not, Driskoll," Kellach said. "Look!"

Driskoll turned to the galeb duhr. The monster was right on top of them. It could have snatched either one of them up with its mouth, if that's what it wanted to do. Yet it didn't. It had stopped, one leg lifted, its blockhead tilted to one side.

"Do you think it's listening to Gryphyll?" Moyra asked.

"I'm not sure, but maybe if we all join in . . ." Kellach trailed off, and he quickly picked up Gryphyll's melody. Moyra joined them, her voice light and airy. Driskoll added his voice last, his gaze glued to the galeb duhr.

The boulder monster no longer looked fierce. It gently rocked from side to side, a soft hum thrumming from it. Its black mouth grew smaller, and its eyes lost some of their glitter.

They hummed louder.

The galeb duhr swayed and swayed and swayed.

"It's working!" Driskoll shouted above their humming.

"How long do we have to keep humming?" Moyra asked between a hum, then started again.

"Until it goes away, I guess," Kellach said.

Suddenly a low, mournful sound erupted from the galeb duhr. The monster leaned back its head, like a wolf baying at the moon, and a deep, strong voice rose above their own. The sound roared above the trees and echoed off the cliff, sad and soft and powerful all at the same time.

Driskoll stopped humming first, then Kellach, then Moyra, and finally Gryphyll. They listened to the galeb duhr's low, steady roar as the monster sang to the sky and the clouds above.

Then the black hole of its mouth closed, and the galeb duhr lowered its head. Its coal-black eyes glittered again, but with tears now, not anger. Then the galeb duhr sank to the ground, and the earth shuddered beneath its weight.

Moyra stepped forward. "That was beautiful," she said. She walked up to the galeb duhr and touched its warm, solid surface.

"Can you understand me? Does your song mean something to your kind?"

The galeb duhr nodded, its head now on level with Moyra's. Its cavernous mouth opened, and it spoke. "It does," said the galeb duhr. Its low, gravelly voice caused the ground to tremble again. Driskoll could feel the vibrations tickle his feet.

"We'd love to hear about it," Moyra said, sitting cross-legged on the ground before the rocky beast.

The galeb duhr shifted and sighed, the hot breeze of its breath rushing across their faces.

"My kind, as you call it, is one of the oldest creatures to roam the earth. You might have seen many of us over the years, but we blend in so perfectly with our surroundings, that you could walk right on by and not even notice.

"But we like it that way," the galeb duhr continued. "We like to be anonymous, to live out our lives as we should."

It paused. Its mouth crumbled and a drop of water trickled from one eye. "Every so often, creatures, such as yourselves, decide to cut into us, not realizing that we are living, breathing beings. Many of my kind have been killed in this way."

"That's so sad!" Moyra said. She looked behind her and waved Kellach and Driskoll to join her on the ground. Driskoll resheathed his sword, then they walked forward and each took a seat on either side of Moyra. Locky popped his head out from Kellach's robes, and Gryphyll stretched out on his belly beside Driskoll and rested his chin in his hands.

"But why would they cut into a big rock like you?" Driskoll asked.

"My kind usually lives high in the mountains, where many

gems and other riches can be found. Many beings go in search of those gems, and they destroy many galeb duhrs in the process."

No one said a word as they thought about the galeb duhr's plight.

"So what brings you here, in the forest below the mountains?" Moyra asked.

"Peace," the galeb duhr admitted. "Here the rocks are too small for beings to trifle with. I have left my home in the mountains for refuge here in the forest."

Something occurred to Driskoll. "You used to live in the mountains? High up in the mountains? Like toward the top?"

"I did, indeed," the galeb duhr gurgled.

"You wouldn't happen to have met any . . ." Driskoll hesitated. "Well, any silver dragons on your mountaintop, would you?"

"Why, of course," the galeb duhr said, as if it were the most natural thing in the world.

Kellach, Driskoll, and Moyra sat up straighter. Even Gryphyll rolled over, stood at Moyra's side, and placed a hand on her shoulder.

"You mean," Driskoll said, "you can tell us where to find one?"

"I don't know where, exactly, you might find a silver dragon," the galeb duhr said slowly. "Silver dragons are hard to find. They don't like to reveal themselves, for long ago, they were hunted and kept as pets, chained to live below the mountains. I recall seeing quite a few silver dragons captured while I still lived there, and it was a very sad sight. Silver dragons are so peaceful, and they believe that good is in everyone. People who wished to capture them used this very trait against them."

The galeb duhr sighed once more, its breath rustling the leaves on the trees.

"How many times I wished that I were faster, that I could have helped the silver dragons." The galeb duhr lowered its head, its eyes glittering at them. "What business do you have with the dragons, if you don't mind my asking?"

"We have something important of theirs to return," Moyra said. "We don't mean them any harm."

"No, I don't believe that you do. You're not like the other creatures I've seen who have brought death and destruction with them. I sense something more in you. A higher purpose, perhaps?"

"Perhaps," Kellach said. "We only know that our purpose right now is to protect the people of our town by returning a medallion once created by a silver dragon. If it were to fall into the wrong hands, the consequences could be dreadful."

"Ah!" the galeb duhr exclaimed. "And someone has entrusted you with this task, so you must be trustworthy. Indeed, I shall tell you all I know about the silver dragons, and I hope that you have success in finding them."

Moyra, Kellach, Driskoll, and Gryphyll gathered more closely around the galeb duhr as it slowly began to explain the ways of the silver dragons.

　　　　　　　🕮　🕮　🕮　🕮　🕮

"I can't believe you didn't bring a blanket!" Driskoll complained, his teeth chattering.

"Well, I can't believe you didn't think to bring a cloak!" Kellach returned, his teeth clicking together.

Moyra didn't say a word as she, Driskoll, Kellach, and

Gryphyll made their way across snowy terrain. Not sure how Locky would react to such cold weather, Kellach had wrapped his familiar in a wool scarf and nestled the mechanical dragon in his pack.

Driskoll breathed heavily, and his breath plumed in the air in front of his face. Since they'd left the galeb duhr four days earlier, they'd climbed steadily upward. Now, the snow that had once seemed so far away had become the only world they knew. No matter what he did, globs of snow still managed to sneak into Driskoll's boots, numbing his toes and dampening his woolen socks. The chill air stung his cheeks and froze his ears, for along with a cloak, Driskoll had also forgotten to bring a hat.

Driskoll squinted against the brightness of the snow, even though the sun hid behind the clouds. The whiteness stretched as far as he could see, blending with the dull light gray of the sky. The higher they had climbed, the colder it had gotten. Eventually, they'd put on every last piece of clothing they'd packed. Now their packs were lighter, but for some reason, heavier.

Perhaps because of the snow they were sludging through, Driskoll thought as he hoisted his pack more firmly in place.

Driskoll looked back and noticed that Moyra's lips had turned blue. Her skin looked, well, it looked rather lavender, a pretty color, really. Just not on a human face.

"Hey, Moyra!" Driskoll called to her. "Are you okay?"

"I'm fine," she said, tromping through the snow. "At least you boys have warm boots. It never occurred to me that we would run into a blizzard up here."

"I don't think this is quite a blizzard," Kellach said. "Blizzards have incredibly strong winds and—"

"I'll tell you what to do with your strong winds. Why don't you blow it—"

"Why are you arguing?" Gryphyll broke in cheerfully. "It's a wonderful adventure we're having. No reason to argue."

"We're not arguing." Moyra sighed.

Driskoll looked at the little troll, or whatever Gryphyll was, and he noticed that Gryphyll didn't seem to be affected by the cold, even though he wore no more clothing than what he had when they'd started.

How strange.

"Hey, Kell," said Moyra. "Couldn't you conjure us up a bunch of hats or gloves or scarves or something?"

Kellach shook his head. "I can't make anything solid like that just pop out of thin air. I could try to conjure up a fire, but that wouldn't do us much good while we're walking."

"Do we even know where we're walking to?" Moyra asked. "It all looks the same to me."

Driskoll agreed with her. The flat, white land led to more flat, white land. A chilling wind kicked up puffs of snow, adding to the near-white conditions. Driskoll strained his eyes for any sign of a mountain ridge or a break in the whiteness. But the scenery was unending.

He wrapped his jacket more tightly around his neck and scrunched forward to block the wind.

"The galeb duhr told us to just keeping walking upward," Kellach said, "until we found a meadow."

"I'm beginning to wonder if the galeb duhr had all its marbles, um, rocks, or whatever," Driskoll said. A sudden burst of wind sent his jacket fluttering open. Driskoll clutched at the edges and buttoned it closed. "A meadow? Up here in the snow? Not likely."

"Galeb duhr," Gryphyll chirped, "what a nice fellow!"

All three kids looked at Gryphyll like he had lost *his* marbles.

"Aren't you cold?" Driskoll asked.

"Cold?" Gryphyll looked puzzled. "This is wonderful! So fresh! So pure! A treasure! Gryphyll likes the snow!" To prove his point, Gryphyll dived into a particularly large snowdrift. Then he popped back up, sputtered, and laughed.

"It's quite delightful!" he exclaimed.

"Yeah, that's what I'd call it," Moyra grumbled. "Delightful."

Driskoll snickered, and for just a moment, he forgot how cold he was as he watched Gryphyll frolic like a puppy in the snow.

Without warning, the earth erupted in front of them. Snow and ice exploded from the ground, bursting upward. It rained down upon them in a painful downpour.

Driskoll, Moyra, Kellach, and even Gryphyll covered their faces to avoid being scratched by the sharp ice shards that fell from the sky.

"What's happening?" Driskoll heard Moyra ask, but he couldn't see her in the snow and ice that fell around them.

"I don't know!" he called out to her.

A needle of ice struck Driskoll's hand, and he smothered a yelp. He peered at his hand through the snow and saw a drop of blood. Red oozed blood from a long nasty scratch on the side of his palm.

Great, Driskoll thought. Just what I need. And on my sword hand too. Driskoll brought his hand to his mouth to stop the trickle of blood.

And then he saw it.

CHAPTER

18

A frost salamander, in all its ferocious glory.

"Holy potatoes!" Moyra gasped.

"We must have walked over a tunnel to its cave or something," Kellach said, "and it sensed us coming."

Driskoll tried to unsheathe his sword, but his palm stung from the scratch and the cold.

The frost salamander let out a deafening roar, and Driskoll cringed, wishing he could disappear inside his jacket and never come out. The frost salamander looked down at them, its fierce yellow eyes glowing strangely in the white world of snow and ice. The beast resembled a large lizard, with its turquoise, pebbly skin and its extremely long tail. It had six legs, each capped by long talons made of ice.

Perfect for grabbing unsuspecting kids, Driskoll thought.

"What do we do?" Moyra asked.

"Kellach?" Driskoll said, turning to his brother.

"Why are you asking me?" said Kellach, his blond hair whipping about his face.

"Because you're supposed to be in charge!" Driskoll said.

"And I've had lots of experience with frost salamanders?" he asked, not taking his eyes off the beast glaring down at them.

"Fine," Driskoll said. "Then there's only one thing to do."

"What?" Kellach and Moyra shouted at the same time.

"Run!"

Driskoll took off, hoping his small size would be no match for the frost salamander's much larger, and hopefully more clumsy, body.

No such luck.

Driskoll looked over his shoulder. The frost salamander lifted its head and roared, a piercing screech that probably could break glass. Sharp, ugly teeth hung inside its mouth, like a ridge of icicles along the roof of a house.

Driskoll looked back in front of him and ordered his legs to run faster.

But it was too late.

Four icy talons wrapped around his body, and suddenly Driskoll found himself airborne. The ground disappeared beneath his feet, and his boots dangled beyond the icy grip of the frost salamander's talons.

Driskoll struggled to get loose. He pounded against the ice-claw, even tried to lift one. The talons only wrapped more firmly around him. He squirmed and squiggled, trying to turn his body, hoping he'd slip to the ground.

Finally, Driskoll gave up. He clung to the frost salamander's claw and watched a world of white below him. Driskoll guessed he was about as high as the wall around Watchers' Hall. He strained his eyes to see Kellach, Moyra, and Gryphyll, hoping one of them would get away. They were merely dots of purple and blue in the snow to Driskoll, but the frost salamander didn't have any trouble finding them.

"Moyra, watch out!" Driskoll shouted.

"Let go of me you . . . you big, slimy lizard!" Moyra yelled.

Driskoll looked to his right and saw Moyra struggling in the frost salamander's talons. Her legs kicked furiously and her hands pushed the icy bond. She even tried to bite it.

"That's not going to work!" Driskoll called to her.

"Oh, no?" Moyra shouted back. "Then what will?"

"I don't know!" Driskoll yelled. "Let's hope that Kellach escapes, and—"

"Too late!" Moyra said, pointing. "Look!"

Driskoll looked ahead in time to see Kellach turn to face the frost salamander. Kellach lifted his arms, like he was trying to conjure a spell. The frost salamander reached out his middle leg, grabbed Kellach around the waist, and hauled him forward.

"Kellach!" Driskoll shouted below him. "Are you all right?"

Kellach's voice came back, strong and steady. "I'm okay. How about you? Moyra?"

"We're all right!" Moyra shouted. "Where's Gryphyll?"

"I don't know!" Kellach shouted up. "How are we going to get out of here?"

Driskoll looked behind him, and up, up at the face of the frost salamander. At the moment, its mouth was closed, hiding its sharp, pointy teeth.

He turned forward again. "I think if he doesn't eat us right away, we might have a chance."

"That's a big if," Moyra said. "Oh, no!"

Driskoll had already seen it. Gryphyll's legs stuck up out of the snow, waggling back and forth.

"He might as well wave a flag and announce where he is!" Driskoll said.

With one of its free claws, the frost salamander plucked Gryphyll from the snow, holding his legs between two icy talons.

"Oh dear, oh dear!" Gryphyll's voice floated up to them.

"Gryphyll!" Moyra cried.

The frost salamander dropped Gryphyll in the snow and reached for him again. This time, it bound Gryphyll in its fist, just like the rest of them.

"He's all right, Moyra," Kellach's voice came from below. "He's here next to me. He's just stunned, that's all."

"Quite right, quite right," Gryphyll's voice drifted up.

"Kellach, where do you think he's taking us?" Driskoll called down to his brother.

"Oh, I don't know," Kellach's voice came from below. "Maybe somewhere like—his ice cave!"

"Can't you put a spell on him or something?" Moyra shouted back.

"Yeah, if only my hands weren't pinned to my sides, that would be a great idea."

"Just asking," Moyra mumbled.

"Do you think he plans to eat us?" Driskoll shouted to anyone.

"It's a pretty good bet," said Kellach.

"Oh dear, oh dear," Gryphyll whimpered.

Driskoll's head began to throb. The frost salamander marched across the snow silently, moving its arms up and down. Its icy breath curled down the collar of Driskoll's jacket, and Driskoll realized that he couldn't stop shaking. His stomach roiled, and bile rose in his throat.

He swallowed hard. Great! Now I'm going to throw up! he thought.

He looked at Moyra and noticed how pale she was. She'd also grown very quiet.

Driskoll gripped the ice talon that bound his chest and held on. He closed his eyes and tried not to imagine what waited for them at the frost salamander's lair.

CHAPTER

19

"This is great, just swell," said Driskoll.

"Will you be quiet?" Kellach said. "At least he didn't eat us right away."

"That makes me feel so much better." Driskoll squirmed inside the icy hollow.

"Well, it should," Kellach countered. "At least now we have some time to figure out how to get out of this mess."

Driskoll felt the cold seep into his body. Wiggling wasn't only a way to try to get loose from the icy nook. It was also a way to keep warm.

As he wiggled, Driskoll looked around and tried to see anything that might help them escape. Nothing but a long tunnel of ice stretched out in front of him. The walls were about twenty feet high, high enough for the frost salamander to stand upright. The icy walls gave off a dull, bluish-gray glow. The walls were smooth except for slight hollows set at regular intervals.

The hollows, as they'd quickly found out, were for storing food.

Kellach, Moyra, Gryphyll, and Driskoll now waited, each in his and her own hollow, covered with ice. Driskoll grimaced as he remembered the frost salamander shoving him into the hollow, then breathing on him and encasing him in ice. Only his head remained free.

Probably so it can see us and decide which one to eat, Driskoll thought dimly.

"Why didn't he eat us right away?" Moyra asked.

"Frost salamanders like to eat their food frozen," Gryphyll said gleefully. "Isn't this fun? Wait until I tell the boys back home."

"What boys?" Moyra asked, wiggling away.

"I don't know," Gryphyll said. "That's what the fellows at the Skinned Cat always say when they've done something particularly fascinating."

"Oh, now I feel much better," Driskoll said. "So basically, the frost salamander is putting us on ice until we're human icicles?"

"Yes, Driskoll!" Gryphyll said. "And then we'll be all cold and crunchy and—"

"I get the idea," Driskoll said. He struggled more urgently inside his ice cocoon.

Driskoll looked over and noticed that Kellach wasn't doing much struggling at all. In fact, Kellach looked like he was sleeping. His body was totally relaxed, his eyes were completely closed, and his head leaned against the ice wall.

Or maybe he'd passed out!

"Kell! Hey, Kellach!" Driskoll yelled. "Are you okay? Wake up! Hey! Wake up!"

Kellach's head snapped forward, and he glared at his brother. "I'm trying to do some conjuring here. Do you mind?"

"Would you like to share your conjuring idea with us?" Driskoll asked sharply.

"I don't want to get your hopes up. That's why I didn't say anything."

"Get our hopes up! Please!" Moyra said.

Kellach hesitated. "Well, I think I might be able to cast a spell us up some fire."

"Fire?" Driskoll said.

"Yes, as in to melt ice with? Get it?"

"Of course!" Driskoll said. "You can do that! I've seen you do that!"

"Yes, but I've always done it with arm gestures. I've never tried to cast a spell without raising my arms. I feel like I'm trying to walk without legs."

"Is all that arm waving really necessary?"

"I don't know," Kellach said honestly.

Moyra smirked. "I always thought it looked a little silly to me, like 'Ooo! Look at me! I'm a wizard! Ooo!'"

"You'll be happy if all that ooo-ing and ah-ing stuff saves your behind, won't you?"

"Conjure away, my friend," Moyra said, "conjure away."

Driskoll held his breath. At first, Kellach didn't look like he was doing anything more strenuous than taking a nap. His head leaned against the wall, his eyes closed, his whole body lay limp. Only his lips gave him away. They pursed in a thin, grim line, as Kellach concentrated very hard.

Driskoll chanted inside his own head. Fire, fire!

Then suddenly, a small flame sprung to life, right before Kellach's face.

"You did it!" Moyra said.

"Don't get too excited," said Kellach. "I'm not done yet."

"What do you mean?" asked Moyra.

"I have to move the thing, don't I? It's not doing much good sitting in front of my face." Kellach's eyes narrowed, focusing on the flame. Slowly, very slowly, the flame began to move downward until it floated before Kellach's chest.

At first, nothing happened. The ice remained frozen and solid. Then a drop of water rolled down the front of Kellach's cocoon.

"I think it's working!" Driskoll shouted.

A few moments later, Kellach burst through the icy wall and he lurched to the floor.

"You did it!" Moyra yelled.

"Good show, young man," Gryphyll said, as if it had been a simple magic trick and not something that their lives depended on.

"Now how about us?" Driskoll asked.

Kellach centered himself in front of them. He lowered his head and took two deep, steady breaths. Then he raised his head and his arms, and he whisked his hands in the air. Three small flames appeared, one before each of them.

"Kellach," Driskoll said, "you're doing it!"

Driskoll felt the heat of the flame on his face, and slowly his body began to warm. The ice near his chest began to melt, and Driskoll pushed against it with his entire body. At last, he burst through the ice and landed, his sword clattering on the floor beside him.

Driskoll stood quickly and watched as first Moyra, then Gryphyll, popped free and landed on the ground.

"I'll never make fun of your wizard stuff again," Moyra said, breathing deeply as she rolled to her feet. She leaned down and helped Gryphyll up.

"That was great, Kell, really," Driskoll said. He moved his arms and jogged in place. "Everything seems to be working okay."

"I think I'm all right," Moyra said, doing a few deep-knee bends. "Gryphyll? How are you?"

"I'm fine, miss, quite fine," said the troll.

"At least all that training with Zendric is good for something," Kellach said offhandedly. Driskoll saw his brother suppress a grin.

"Now let's get out of here!" Kellach said. "Come on!"

Driskoll and Kellach ran down the tunnel, Moyra close behind, holding on to Gryphyll's hand. The slick floor made running challenging. Driskoll skittered across the ice and tried to steady himself by groping along the tunnel wall. Gryphyll shot past him, laughing as he slid by on the floor. Driskoll helped the little troll up as Kellach and Moyra ran ahead.

Driskoll ran to catch up to them, when suddenly they stopped.

"Keep going!" Driskoll shouted.

A piercing screech ripped through the ice cave. The frost salamander stood in the tunnel, its six-taloned claws scraping the air, its yellow eyes glowing. Its tail flicked back and forth, and its head brushed the roof of the cave. The width of its body totally filled the tunnel, blocking their escape.

"We're trapped!" Driskoll shouted.

CHAPTER

20

"I'll conjure up an obscuring mist!" Kellach yelled above the salamander's screeching. "We'll hide ourselves in the mist and get out of here!"

"Just make it quick!" Moyra yelled back.

The frost salamander whipped its claws at them, first a pair of claws on the right, and then a pair of claws on the left. Driskoll felt the breeze as the claws barely missed him.

"Everyone, get behind me!" Kellach ordered.

Driskoll stumbled past him, Moyra and Gryphyll not far behind. Kellach raised his arms and chanted a few strange words, his voice echoing off the cave walls.

Nothing happened.

Kellach tried again. He chanted more slowly, adding a few more words. Driskoll held his breath and waited for the mist to conceal them.

Nothing.

"What's wrong?" Moyra screamed.

"I don't know!" Kellach said.

"Here's another plan," Driskoll spoke quickly. "This stupid lizard—"

"Salamander," Gryphyll corrected.

"Whatever! It's too big to turn around inside the tunnel. Let's slide beneath its legs. We'll be out of the cave before it's able to turn around and follow."

"That's your plan?" Moyra said.

"Do you have a better one?" Driskoll shot back.

"Good plan!" Moyra yelled. "Let's go!"

Moyra dived to the floor and skidded between the frost salamander's legs. Gryphyll went next, emitting a loud, "Weeee!" as he slid.

The frost salamander screeched, the sound of its voice causing icicles to shake loose from the cave's ceiling.

"Great. Now we have to dodge the frost salamander's claws and falling icicles?" Driskoll said, looking over his shoulder at his brother.

"All the more reason why we need to get out of here," Kellach said. "Driskoll, you next!"

"No, Kellach, you go."

"Driskoll, I'm in charge here. You—hey!"

Driskoll pushed Kellach to the ground and landed on top of him. An icy talon tore through the air above their heads, missing them by inches.

Kellach and Driskoll scrambled to their hands and knees and crawled toward the frost salamander's legs. This time, Driskoll didn't wait for his brother to argue. He pushed Kellach through, kicking him in the behind. Kellach sprawled across the ice, and he slid headfirst between the salamander's legs.

Driskoll scurried as quickly as he could after Kellach. He'd just about cleared the salamander's legs, when something reached out and grabbed him.

"Come on!" Kellach said, hauling Driskoll up by his arm. "We don't have much time before the salamander turns itself around."

The frost salamander's tail thrashed crazily back and forth and Kellach leaped over it and took off down the tunnel. Driskoll tried to time his leap so he wouldn't get tangled up in the salamander's tail. He counted one, two, three, then he ran and jumped and fell down hard, not on the ice, but on greenish-blue speckled skin.

"Hey—whoa!" Driskoll shouted, clinging to the rough surface of the tail. The frost salamander screeched again and stomped its feet, bringing down ice and snow on Driskoll's head. The frost salamander thrashed its tail from side to side, beating it against the wall.

Driskoll wrapped his arms and legs around the tail. He waited for one good thrash—there!

Driskoll let go of the tail and flew through the tunnel.

"Yaaaaa!" he hollered, his arms cartwheeling and his legs kicking. He fell hard against the icy floor and slid another few feet before finally stopping not far from Kellach.

"Well, that's one way of doing it." Kellach chuckled. He skidded back a few steps and helped Driskoll to his feet. Then they stumbled down the tunnel together, clinging to each other, helping each other maintain their balance. Finally they saw the light at the end of the tunnel, and two figures outlined in the tunnel's opening. It was Moyra and Gryphyll.

"What happened?" Moyra asked breathlessly.

"Went for a ride," Driskoll said, panting.

The ground trembled beneath their feet.

"It's coming!" Kellach hollered, dashing out the cave entrance. "Run!"

Moyra, Driskoll, and Gryphyll fled into the clearing outside. It was snowing now and the sky had turned dark and gray. Looking over his shoulder, Driskoll saw the frost salamander barreling out the entrance of the cave, his creepy claws wiggling above his head.

He lowered his head and put everything he had into making his legs move as fast as they could. The snow held him back, sucking at his boots, making him fall face first into the snow. The flakes were falling so hard he couldn't see more than a few feet in front of him.

Driskoll struggled to stand, wiping snow from his mouth and eyes.

"Moyra? Kellach?" he called.

There was no answer.

Footprints splattered the ground in front of him. Driskoll tore through the heavy snow, trying not to imagine the furious monster behind him. He kept his gaze glued to the footprints, using them as a guide. But the tracks were quickly disappearing in the falling snow.

Still running, Driskoll glanced back. He didn't see his brother or Moyra anywhere. All he saw was the frost salamander, gaining ground, getting closer, closer.

Driskoll willed his legs to run faster.

After only a few steps the ground beneath him opened up. Driskoll swung his arms, desperately trying to grab hold of something.

The only thing his fingers felt was air.

CHAPTER

21

Driskoll plummeted downward.

He heard nothing but the wind whistling through his ears. He saw nothing but the white ice cliff over which he'd fallen and the gray sky above. He lay on his back, as if his pack pulled him downward. His arms flapped uselessly at his sides, his legs kicked helplessly in the air.

Strangely, Driskoll did not feel scared. Instead, a calm settled over him.

For most definitely, this was it.

It, as in, it's been a nice life; see you later.

Well, at least it had been fun and exciting and—

"Umph!"

Driskoll's senses returned to him in a whoosh.

Something had stopped his fall.

Driskoll sat up carefully and felt beneath him.

The first thing he felt was warmth. His fingers lay atop something very warm and very . . . hairy.

Hairy? Driskoll shook his head. A long strand of hair

blew into his mouth, and Driskoll sputtered and coughed to get it out.

Driskoll looked down and gasped. He sat upon a horse, a beautiful horse.

A beautiful silvery horse, soaring on a gust of air.

"A wind steed!" Driskoll whispered. Driskoll recalled his mother telling him the tale of the wind steeds, each adventure more thrilling than the next. Driskoll had turned each one into his own ballad of courage and daring.

And he never imagined that they were real!

Driskoll held on to the wind steed's silky mane. Snowcapped mountain peaks towered above him, and soft clouds billowed by. The snow had stopped, the clouds had parted, and blue, blue sky soared above. Below, a world of white glittered and sparkled. A few evergreen trees spired up from the snow, their pointy tops reaching toward the sky. A ring of jagged peaks rimmed the horizon, covered with snow. Driskoll tried to see Curston on the other side, but even St. Cuthbert's remained hidden.

Driskoll inhaled deeply. The cool wind felt wonderful against his face, and the wind steed's mane tickled his nose. Driskoll laughed out loud.

The wind steed leaned to the side, and Driskoll looked down and saw the ground coming nearer. Peering around the wind steed's neck, he spotted six spots of color in the snow. Then the wind steed held its wings out to the sides, and it landed, soft but sure.

Driskoll grinned broadly.

"Well, he looks like he's feeling okay," Moyra observed as Driskoll slid from the back of the wind steed.

"Okay? I feel great!" Driskoll patted the wind steed's neck and rubbed her nose. "Isn't she the most beautiful creature you've ever seen?"

"And here I thought I was the most beautiful," Moyra said. "I guess you have a thing for horses?"

Kellach rolled his eyes. "Driskoll's had a thing for flying horses since we were kids."

"Really? I couldn't tell," Moyra said.

"Pretty horses!" Gryphyll said, stroking the mane of hair that adorned one of the wind steed's front legs.

"This isn't just a horse!" Driskoll said. "It's a wind steed!"

Actually, we're asperis, the horse said in a soft, female voice. *My name is Zillia.*

Driskoll stumbled, almost falling over. "You can talk?"

Not exactly, Zillia said gently. As she spoke she nudged Driskoll's hand and Driskoll realized her mouth wasn't moving. But he could hear her voice in his head all the same.

We've learned to communicate telepathically with your kind, as well as with other creatures of the mountains.

"Wind steeds are very intelligent," Driskoll said, looking into the silver horse's big eyes.

The horse laughed, a tinkling sound, like wind chimes. *We try to be. Sometimes it's the only way to stay alive.*

"I think we have you to thank for that," Kellach said. "I'm grateful you rescued us. If you hadn't been there, my friends and I would be splattered all over the place."

"Or lunch for the frost salamander," said Moyra.

The frost salamander? Zillia shook her head. *He's up to his old tricks again, is he?*

"I guess so," said Driskoll. "Although I'm not sure what his old tricks are. He had us iced up in his cave. Looked like he was going to enjoy us for a snack later."

Kellach scoffed. "The frost salamander is just a big bully."

The small herd of four asperis snickered.

"A big bully with really big teeth," Moyra added.

The asperis began throwing their heads back, sending their manes fluttering.

Driskoll reluctantly removed his hand from Zillia's mane, and he walked over to join Kellach, Moyra, and Gryphyll.

"They seem to know a lot about the frost salamander," he said.

"Seems like it," said Moyra. "It sounds like our friendly frosty has been terrorizing the inhabitants of the mountain for years." Changing the subject, she asked, "By the way, what happened to you two back there? Gryphyll and I were running our feet off, and when I turned around, you weren't anywhere near us. Silly me, I didn't see the edge of the cliff until it was too late. By then, Gryphyll and I were both falling pretty fast."

Driskoll nodded. "Same thing happened to me. It was just lucky for us the asperis arrived when they did."

Kellach grinned and cracked his knuckles. "Luck had nothing to do with it."

"What do you mean?" Driskoll asked.

"I mean I summoned these creatures to save your behinds."

"What!" Moyra stomped her foot in the snow. "You can't summon an asperi! Not even Zendric could do that."

Kellach's grin faded just a little. "I can, too!"

As Kellach and Moyra argued, Driskoll observed the four asperis romping in the snow. The asperis had taken them to . . . to a . . . snow meadow, was the only way Driskoll could think to describe it. The smooth flat area was covered with snow, and steep mountains beyond held them in a circle of jagged peaks. In the distance, Driskoll thought he could see a forest of evergreens, but here, nothing grew.

Driskoll turned his attention to Zillia. She was a silvery color, and looking more closely, he discovered that each asperi had a slightly different hue. The steed Moyra had ridden on was slightly lavender. Kellach's was slightly green, a soft emerald. And Gryphyll's was a pale pink. The asperis tossed their heads and flicked their tails, the long lengths of hair flying gracefully around them.

Driskoll still couldn't believe he'd actually ridden an asperi. "Mom would have loved this," he said to Kellach.

"What, freezing our toes off, nearly getting eaten by a frost salamander, and jumping off cliffs?"

"No, the asperis. The wind steeds. Don't you remember the stories she used to tell us?"

Kellach's expression turned thoughtful. "Yeah, Dris, I do. Now, when we see her again, we can tell her what they're really like, huh?"

Although they didn't say it, the thought hung in the air between them: if they ever saw her again.

"Hey!" Moyra said. "I have an idea. Since the asperis seem to know so much about the 'inhabitants' of the mountains, as they called them, perhaps they know where we might find a silver dragon?"

Kellach snapped out of the past and sprang back into the present. "The medallion. Of course! Between being cold and nearly becoming the frost salamander's next meal, I almost forgot why we were here." He felt under his robes to make sure the pouch still hung there.

Moyra tapped her head, "Think, boys! We've got an important mission to accomplish." Turning to Driskoll, she said, "Why don't you ask the asperis about the silver dragons, since you seem to have such a connection with them?"

"Sure!" Driskoll said.

The group walked over to the small herd of asperis. They watched the horses romp a bit more, then Driskoll said, as politely and respectfully as possible, "Excuse me! Um, excuse me!"

Finally the asperis heard them, and they trotted over.

"First, thank you so much for saving us," Driskoll said, bowing slightly. "My friends and I don't know how we will ever repay you."

"So nice, so nice!" Gryphyll added. "A treasure!"

He drew the attention of Zillia. The asperi gazed at him closely, then her large, brown eyes widened. She snickered and shook her head, her mane fluttering around her neck, as if to shake off an absurd thought.

It was an honor, she said.

"An honor?" Driskoll said, surprised. "Well, um, I don't know about all that. But, you see, we're actually on a mission."

Of course you are. The asperi's voice was light and sweet.

"You know?"

Well, we didn't think you were up here in the mountains, battled frost salamanders—

137

"—and galeb duhrs!" Gryphyll added.

And galeb duhrs too? The asperi shook her mane again. *Well, you have been rather busy, haven't you?*

"Yes, ma'am, we have," Driskoll said. Ma'am? he thought to himself. Do you call horses 'ma'am'?

Moyra nudged him. "Go on, ask her!"

Driskoll flung an impatient look over his shoulder, then he turned back to the asperi. Zillia looked at him with her big soft eyes.

Driskoll suddenly felt all flustered, and his tongue didn't seem to know how to form any words.

Zillia nudged Driskoll's arm. *What do you need?*

Kellach stepped up. "We need your help."

"Yes!" Driskoll finally said. He shook himself to clear his head. Wind steed or not, mythical creature or not, they had an important quest of their own to complete. "We need to find a silver dragon. We thought that maybe, since you seem to know the mountains so well and the creatures that live here, maybe you might know where we could find one."

Zillia moved her gaze from Driskoll and stared at Gryphyll. She narrowed her eyes and tilted her head. To Driskoll it seemed like the asperi was sizing up the silly toad.

Gryphyll sneezed, and the asperi let loose a tinkling laugh.

Silver dragons? And what might you children need with a silver dragon?

Kellach untied the pouch at his waist and pulled out the medallion. The silver glinted in the bright sun of the snowy mountaintop, the amethyst eyes giving off a peculiar glow.

Driskoll remembered the effect the medallion had had on him, and he turned away. Moyra did the same. Gryphyll, he realized, did not.

"Oh, how brilliant!" Gryphyll said.

"This is the medallion of the silver dragon," Kellach explained. He held it in his palm and walked toward the asperis. "We have been invested by the power of the Knights of the Silver Dragon to return this medallion to its rightful owner, the silver dragon who created it."

I would like to help you, my friends, but I'm afraid that won't be possible, Zillia explained, while the other asperis gathered around her.

"Why not?" Moyra asked.

You see, the silver dragons no longer exist.

22

W hat do you mean?" Kellach asked. "We were told that the silver dragons lived here, up in the mountains."

Zillia looked at each of them in turn. Her glance paused briefly on Gryphyll, before she continued. *The silver dragons did, indeed, live here long ago, but we have not seen one in a very long time.*

"Then they could still live here?" Moyra asked. "Maybe they're just hiding."

It's possible. Silver dragons are solitary creatures. They are happiest being by themselves. At one time, we used to see a silver dragon or two, soaring through the sky above the mountaintops. But we have not seen one now in a very long time. A very long time.

"But that doesn't mean that they don't exist," Moyra insisted. "I mean, after all, we've never seen asperis before today, but here you are."

The asperi whinnied. *She's a sharp one, isn't she?*

"You have no idea," Driskoll said. "If there were silver dragons still around, where would they most likely be?"

The asperi blinked its wide eyes. Once again, she looked around the small group, then she turned her head to her asperi companions. Moyra, Driskoll, and Kellach waited to hear what they said next.

"If the asperi could tell us how to find the silver dragons," Driskoll whispered, "we'd be that much closer to returning the medallion and completing the quest."

"I do so hope they help us!" Gryphyll added loudly.

Zillia's head whipped around and she stared at Gryphyll. Gryphyll beamed back at her. Something seemed to settle in the asperi's mind. She shook her head, her mane of silver-white waving gloriously. *We won't tell you about the silver dragons.*

Driskoll's stomach dipped. "But—"

Zillia lifted a hoof and pawed the air. *Instead, we will take to the last place we've seen them.*

Driskoll's jaw dropped. "You'll take us?"

Zillia nodded.

"Yes!" Moyra said, clapping once.

"I don't know how we'd be able to thank you," said Kellach.

Complete your task, young man. That is all the thanks we need.

Driskoll, Moyra, and Kellach looked at each other and grinned.

"So nice to help! So nice!" Gryphyll joined in. "A treasure, it is! A treasure!"

Zillia lowered her head before Driskoll, inviting him to climb onto her back. Driskoll grasped a fistful of her mane, careful not to pull too harshly. He lifted a leg and tried to fling it over

Zillia's back. But his sword got in the way, and he fell over, landing on his back.

"It was a lot easier getting on you when I was falling through the sky," Driskoll grumbled. He picked himself up and brushed the snow from his pants. He tried it again, this time hopping on one foot as he flung the other leg over the asperi's back. He clung to Zillia's neck and hauled himself up, half sprawled, half sitting across her.

Driskoll glanced over to Kellach and Moyra. Kellach was already seated, his legs hugging his green asperi's sides. Moyra had joined her hands to form a step for Gryphyll, and she gently raised him onto his asperi's back. Then it was her turn. Driskoll groaned as Moyra nimbly climbed on board, her leg sailing gracefully over the asperi and her arms hoisting her onto its back. Show off, he thought.

Driskoll grasped Zillia's silvery mane and clenched his legs around Zillia's sides. The wind steed started to trot, then she broke into an all-out gallop. Driskoll bounced along, grinning from ear to ear.

Then the asperi leaped off the cliff.

And they were airborne.

"Yaaaaahhhoooo!" Driskoll shouted. The snow meadow fell away below them, and the peaks of the mountains rose sharply in front of them. Once again, they flew among the clouds.

Driskoll tried to absorb every sensation so he would never forget what it felt like to ride on the back of the wind steed. The asperi's mane fluttered across his face and tickled his nose. Her fur was soft beneath his hands, and he could feel the rhythm of her heart beneath his thighs. The cool breeze brushed Driskoll's cheeks.

A tall mountain loomed before them, its rugged, rocky peak dusted with snow. Zillia lifted her front legs, and they soared over the mountain and glided down the other side. A deep chasm opened up beneath them, and Driskoll gripped Zillia a bit more tightly. A stream cut through the large, jagged hole, bubbling and frothing over boulders of snow and rock. A blanket of snow still lay over the land, and pine trees dotted the white in random patterns of green.

They continued to fly through clouds, full of snow that had yet to fall. Looking to his left, Driskoll saw Moyra and Gryphyll on their wind steeds, and to his right, Kellach sat upon his. Kellach looked over at the same moment and smiled hugely, and Driskoll waved.

Driskoll sensed when the asperi began to slow and descend. He looked down and spied a valley between the mountains, and what looked like a large patch of greenery. As the asperi got closer, Driskoll could just make out the colorful heads of flowers.

Zillia landed lightly and trotted a few steps before she stopped. Flowers waved on their longs stems and brushed against Zillia's legs, their petals a mix of red, yellow, and orange.

"A meadow!" Driskoll exclaimed. "In the middle of the snow!"

Of course. Where else would a silver dragon be?

The asperis with Kellach, Moyra, and Gryphyll landed not far from Driskoll. He watched as they slid off the backs of their horses. Gryphyll kicked his stubby legs, and Moyra held him about the waist, helping him to the ground.

Driskoll didn't want to leave Zillia. He knew he would never see her again. He hugged her neck, then slid off her back and joined his friends in the meadow.

"It's amazing!" Moyra said. "Who would have thought that grass and flowers could grow in such a cold place."

"Haven't you noticed?" Kellach said, his blond hair swept back from his face. "It's not cold here at all."

Kellach was right. The air was definitely warmer. Driskoll inhaled deeply, and the air smelled like flowers.

"It's like springtime," he said.

That it is. Zillia nodded. *You must never forget that the silver dragons are wonderful, peaceful creatures. Only a silver dragon could create such beauty in such a desolate place.*

"So a silver dragon does live here?" Kellach asked.

A silver dragon lived here once, long ago. As I said, we have not seen one in many years. Driskoll noted that Zillia once more looked at Gryphyll, then she turned back to Kellach. *We wish you success with your quest. Now, we must be off.*

Driskoll walked up to Zillia and stroked her mane one last time. "We are forever grateful," he said solemnly. The words didn't seem enough. "I'll never forget you."

You'll be fine, Zillia assured him.

Driskoll flung an arm around her neck and hugged her for one brief moment. Then he withdrew and stepped back. Zillia whinnied softly and nodded, then she turned and trotted away from them. Her trot became a gallop, and she leaped into the sky, her companions close behind.

Driskoll watched until they were just specks in the sky, then he turned to Kellach and Moyra, who were trying really hard not to laugh.

"Okay, okay, I know. I'm a big baby," Driskoll said.

"I think it's sweet," Moyra said, laughing at last.

Kellach shook his head. "You and your wind steeds."

"Are you done making fun of me?" Driskoll said, but his words had no heat. He knew he would have reacted the same way if Kellach or Moyra had behaved as he had around the asperis. "If you haven't forgotten, we do have a silver dragon to find."

Driskoll walked away and crossed the field, his hands outstretched, feeling the tips of the flowers as they brushed his fingers. "I guess the silver dragon is here somewhere, but where?"

Moyra looked around. "Do you see a rock? Or a tree? Anything that might be like a door?"

Driskoll continued to stroll through the meadow, searching for some sign of a dragon. Red and purple and orange and yellow burst from the flowers around him. He gazed across the field, and he could just make out the edge of the meadow, where the flowers ended and the snow began.

"It can't be far," he said. "This meadow isn't that big."

Gryphyll chased a butterfly through the flowers, his cheerful voice drifting on the warm springlike breeze.

"I'm sure the asperis knew what they were talking about," said Kellach. "There has to be something here."

"Butterfly! Butterfly! Pretty, pretty butterfly!" Gryphyll chanted.

"I agree," Moyra said, "but where?"

Driskoll stopped watching Gryphyll and turned to Kellach. "What do you think, Kell? Do you sense anything?"

"Butterfly! Pretty!" Gryphyll exclaimed.

Driskoll ignored him.

"Kell?"

"I'm sensing, okay?" Kellach said.

Driskoll shrugged and decided to do his own sensing. He wandered a bit farther on his own, daydreaming about asperis and flying over mountains and writing ballads to tell about it.

"Pretty butterfly!" Gryphyll said once again.

Driskoll shook his head and turned to the little troll. "Gryphyll, why don't you help us find the silver dragon and stop chasing butterflies?"

Driskoll looked the other way. "Gryphyll?"

The flowers waved in the breeze, their heads nodding gently. Driskoll strained his eyes. No head popped up out of the flowers. No arms reached up to grab butterflies. No voice jabbered away.

"Gryphyll!"

CHAPTER

23

Moyra ran up to Driskoll. "Where did he go?"

"I don't know!" Driskoll said. "One minute he was over there, chasing butterflies, and the next minute, he just disappeared."

"We have to find him!" Moyra cried.

"I'm sure he's all right," Kellach said.

Moyra didn't listen. She ran in the direction that Driskoll had pointed, the area where he had last seen Gryphyll.

Driskoll and Kellach started after her. They heard her cry out, and her body pitched forward, her arms stabbing the air above her head. Then she was gone.

"Moyra!" Kellach yelled. He and Driskoll raced across the field.

"I'm okay, I'm okay!" she called out. "I'm over here!"

Kellach and Driskoll ran in the direction of her voice. They saw Moyra on her hands and knees among the flowers. A dark hole gaped in front of her.

"He's in here!" Moyra said over her shoulder, her red hair falling into her eyes. She pushed back the strands with an impatient hand. "I can see him! Well, I can see his eyes at least. Take a look."

Driskoll and Kellach joined Moyra on the ground and peered into the hole. At first, Driskoll didn't see much of anything but darkness. Slowly two light purple spots appeared.

"Gryphyll?" Driskoll called. "Is that you?"

The purple spots blinked. "Why, of course! Took a little tumble, I did." Gryphyll giggled.

"We've got to get him out of there," Moyra exclaimed.

"We will," Kellach assured her. "Let me see if I can try a levitation spell, okay?"

"Great!" Moyra said. She shouted down the hole, "Don't worry, Gryphyll! Kellach's going to try to make you float in the air and come back up through the hole. Are you ready?"

"I have nowhere else to go but up!" Gryphyll chirped.

Kellach closed his eyes and scrunched his face.

"Gryphyll!" Moyra called down. "Are you floating yet?"

"Can't say that I am, miss!" he called back.

"Kellach, try harder!" Moyra urged.

Kellach's face scrunched up even more, his lips pursed, his nose red. Driskoll tried not to laugh.

Finally Kellach let out a huge breath and fell over, panting. "It's not working! I don't know why! I've never had trouble with that spell before."

Moyra scoffed and started digging in her pack. "Thank the gods I thought to bring some rope. You know what my dad always says . . ."

"You never know when you're going to need some rope," Driskoll intoned. He'd heard it a hundred times before.

"That's right," Moyra said, triumphantly producing a length of rope from her pack.

She leaned over the hole and shouted, "We're going to toss down a rope, Gryphyll. Tie it around yourself, and we'll pull you up, all right?"

"Sure, miss. I'll do as you say," Gryphyll said.

Moyra lay on her stomach and dangled the rope through the hole. "Do you have it?" she asked Gryphyll.

"I can't reach it miss! Too short, I am!"

"Holy potatoes!" Moyra exploded. She wrenched the rope back up. "I guess I'm going to have to go in after him."

"No, you're not," Kellach said.

"Just watch me." Before either one of them could stop her, she rolled over, placed both feet into the hole, and pushed off.

And only went down waist-high.

Moyra growled. "I'm stuck! The hole is too narrow!"

Driskoll couldn't help laughing this time. "I think I like you like that, Moyra," he said.

"Would you just stuff it and help me out of here?"

"It looks to me like you're already stuffed." Kellach laughed.

"You boys are hysterical, do you know that? Now quit laughing and give me a hand."

Driskoll and Kellach eyed each other, then nodded.

Kellach snickered. "Okay, but only because you asked so nicely."

Driskoll and Kellach each grabbed an arm, then they pulled and tugged until Moyra popped free. All three of them spilled to the ground.

"Gee, that was fun," Driskoll joked. "Can we do it again sometime?"

Moyra glared at him, then crawled back to the hole. "Gryphyll? Are you still okay?"

"Right as rain, miss!" his voice drifted up. "Just me and the worms down here!"

"We'll be right there to get you. Sit tight!" Moyra instructed. Turning to Kellach and Driskoll, she said, "We're going to have to make the hole wider."

"With what?" Driskoll said, looking around. "I didn't pack a shovel."

Moyra held up her hands, then pointedly placed them on the ground. Looking over her shoulder, she shot them a meaningful glare.

"I guess we'd better do as she says," Driskoll said.

"Yeah, you know what she'll say if we make her angry," Kellach said.

"Holy potatoes!" Driskoll said, imitating Moyra's voice. He plopped on the ground beside her, and Kellach plopped on the other side. "Okay, let's start digging!"

They dug for many minutes, flinging clumps of dirt over their shoulders and exchanging a few not-so-nice words. Moyra wiped her forehead with her arm and left a large smudge of dirt across her brow. Driskoll was sure he was just as dirt-speckled as she was. Kellach, on the other hand, had not a smudge on him. He wasn't even sweating.

Driskoll shrugged and kept digging. Suddenly, the earth gave way beneath his hands, and he tumbled forward. Kellach grabbed the collar of his tunic and pulled him back before he fell into the hole.

"Perfect!" Moyra scrambled over the edge and disappeared.

"Moyra!" Kellach shouted after her. She didn't respond right away, and he called again. Finally, her voice came up through the hole.

"I'm okay, it's not that far of a drop."

"How's Gryphyll?" Driskoll asked.

"I don't know." Her voice sounded thin and reedy.

"What do you mean, you don't know?" Kellach said.

"What I mean is that he's not here."

"Well, where is he?"

"He must have waddled off somewhere," Moyra said.

"Curse it," Kellach muttered. He looked up at Driskoll. "Well, it looks like we're going in."

Driskoll grinned. "Looks that way. Besides, I didn't have anything else to do today."

"No, me neither," Kellach replied, swinging his legs over the edge. "Just finding a silver dragon and trying to save the world."

"Or our part of it," Driskoll agreed.

"See you down there," Kellach said. He pushed off and disappeared into the ground.

Driskoll did the same, not even questioning why they were going after the little toad. He fell through the hole and landed with an unceremonious hrumph. Rolling to his feet, he blinked until his eyes adjusted to the dim light. Walls of dirt curved on each side of him, and roots hung free from the dirt ceiling above. If he stood on tiptoe and reached up as far as his fingers would go, Driskoll was sure he could have tugged on the roots, the ceiling was that low. Cool air kissed his skin, and a scent of moss and earth drifted around him. Brushing dirt from his hands, he spied Kellach and Moyra a few feet away.

"There's a tunnel here," Moyra said. She pointed down a dark shaft. "He must have wandered off this way."

"Why would he do that?" Driskoll asked. "He knew we were coming to get him."

"Who knows what goes on in the mind of a . . . well, of a gryphyll," Moyra said as she started down the tunnel.

"I wish we had a candle or something," Driskoll said. "Hey, Kell, why don't you summon up a flame, like you did in the ice cave?"

"I don't think that's necessary," Kellach replied. "Look. I think there's a light at the end there."

Driskoll peered forward, and he saw a speck of gray in the darkness. The deeper into the tunnel they walked, the bigger and brighter the gray speck became. Driskoll looked behind, but he couldn't see where they'd come from. The dirt walls seemed to close in behind them, giving them no other choice but to move forward.

They walked farther, and the light became brighter. Driskoll saw bugs scurry up the dirt walls, and a centipede slithered behind a rock. And Gryphyll had been right—worms poked their heads out of holes in the walls, then quickly dodged back inside.

They quickened their steps and hurried down the tunnel, anxious to find Gryphyll and continue their quest.

"Gryphyll? Gryphyll, are you in there?" Moyra called. Driskoll made out more details of the tunnel. Its ragged walls rippled on either side of them, as if a giant mole or worm had dug the tunnel using claws. Or its body, if it were a worm.

Suddenly Moyra bounded forward, racing toward the opening at the tunnel's end, calling Gryphyll's name.

"Moyra, wait!" Kellach shouted after her. "You don't know what's in there!"

Moyra didn't listen.

She disappeared into the room, into the light.

And then she screamed.

CHAPTER

24

D riskoll and Kellach propelled themselves as quickly as possible through the tunnel until they stood in the opening.

And there, they saw what had made Moyra cry out.

It wasn't an ormyrr or a galeb duhr. It wasn't a frost salamander or even some hideous underground worm.

No, it was a silver dragon.

The silver dragon stood on its hind legs, its wings unfolded in all its dragon glory, its tail swishing back and forth lazily. Its silver scales sparkled in the light of the cave, which came from a dozen golden lanterns placed about the room.

But perhaps more than anything, the eyes drew Driskoll's attention. Purple eyes gazed upon them with a look that Driskoll couldn't quite identify. A look of friendship? Kindness? Curiosity?

And then, suddenly, it hit him.

Purple eyes.

Purple eyes!

"Holy potatoes!" he breathed, and this time, he wasn't mocking Moyra. He meant it with ever fiber of his being.

"I know!" Moyra said, "A silver dragon! Pretty unbeliev-able, huh?"

"That's not it," Driskoll said.

"Are you nuts?" Kellach said. "Of course it is!"

"No, no, I know it's a silver dragon," Driskoll said.

"Well, what, then?" Kellach said.

"It's his eyes," said Driskoll. "Look at them!"

"I know!" said Moyra. "They're amazing."

"And purple," Kellach added, "just like on the medallion."

"Is that the only place you remember seeing purple eyes?" Driskoll said, hoping to lead them to the same conclusion that he'd just reached.

He knew when the discovery hit each of them. Kellach's eyes narrowed, as if he were studying a newly unearthed species. And Moyra—her eyes lit with surprise and pleasure.

"Gryphyll?" she said, turning to the dragon.

The dragon nodded, fluttered his wings, and smiled. "A trea-sure, miss, a treasure! It is I, your dear little toad of a friend." His voice was deep and low, mellow but authoritative, all at the same time.

"But how can this be?" Moyra asked.

"I don't understand," said Kellach. "If you're really Gryphyll, and you're really a silver dragon, why did you make us go through all this? Why not just announce yourself, take the medallion, and be done with it?"

Gryphyll sighed and lowered his head. "So true, so true, young sir! And Zendric has taught you well, I see. He has taught you to question everything, including me." He nodded his head sagely. "Quite wise, of course, quite wise. But please, come in.

Come in!" The dragon waved a hand, indicating his cave. "Make yourselves comfortable while I explain everything."

Driskoll didn't blame Kellach for being skeptical. He hardly believed it himself. Yet as they walked deeper into Gryphyll's lair—for that's what he assumed it was—he recalled odd Gryphyll moments. Like how Gryphyll loved the cold and the snow and didn't need warm clothing. Like how Gryphyll had looked at the silver dragon medallion when he and Moyra had looked away. Like how Zillia had stared at Gryphyll, as if she'd seen him before. At the time, Driskoll had thought Gryphyll was just strange to her. Now he suspected that she had figured out who—or what—he was: a silver dragon in hiding.

Kellach, Driskoll, and Moyra made themselves comfortable on a few stone ledges that rimmed the room. Gryphyll sat in the middle of the cave and folded his wings behind him. His purple eyes glowed, and his mouth curved into a smile.

"It all began with the Sundering of the Seal, you see," he began.

"You mean, the time when evil was released back into Curston," Kellach said.

Gryphyll nodded. "Even here, in the mountains, we were aware that evil had returned to the world. Many of us decided to battle the monsters and drive them back behind the seal." Gryphyll paused, and a sad note crept into his voice. "A sad time that was, yes indeed. Many of us died, you know."

"Oh, Gryphyll!" Moyra exclaimed.

Gryphyll continued. "I had flown to Watchers' Hall to offer my services." He shook his head. "But I arrived too late. By the time I got there, evil had already overcome the city. The monsters

157

set Watchers' Hall on fire, and the smoke quickly overcame me. I felt myself falling out of the sky."

Driskoll leaned forward, drinking in this first-hand account of the Sundering. Zendric rarely talked about it, except in terms of how it affected Curston at present. As an aspiring bard, Driskoll found Gryphyll's story fascinating.

"The next thing I remember, I was lying on the ground, buried in the ruins of Watchers' Hall. Most of the battles were over, and the evil had moved on. I stumbled to my feet, and it was then that I realized that my medallion had fallen from my neck. I searched the rubble, but I couldn't find it anywhere." He took a deep breath. "I've been living in the prison, ever since, searching for it."

"What do you mean?" Kellach said. "My father is the captain of the watch. He'd know if a dragon had been living there."

"Yes, Torin," Gryphyll said. "I know him well. Good man, good man!"

"There is no way my father would know you and not tell us," Kellach said, "He knows that we've been inducted into the old order, into the Knights of the Silver Dragon."

Gryphyll smiled hugely then, his dragon's teeth glistening.

"I am most pleased that the old order is being restored," Gryphyll said. "A treasure, indeed! And I couldn't be more proud of the first three true knights to be inducted."

Kellach gasped. "You mean—"

"Yes, my friends," Gryphyll said. "Your quest. You've completed the quest." He turned to Moyra. "You, miss, with your fiery spirit and kind heart. You have no idea how much you will accomplish with those traits."

Driskoll saw Moyra, very uncharacteristically, blush.

"And you, sir," Gryphyll continued, turning to Driskoll. "So young, yet so loyal and always willing to help, even when you're not sure what to do. Very admirable. One day, I am sure, you will be a strong warrior and an excellent bard."

Driskoll lowered his head and felt heat flush his cheeks. Geesh! he thought silently. How embarrassing! Now I'm blushing!

"And then we come to Kellach," Gryphyll continued, gazing at Kellach warmly. "You, my friend, will one day be an amazing wizard. I sense it. You are only just now beginning to realize your powers. Follow Zendric. Learn from him. It will be up to you to one day pass on the old ways."

Unlike Moyra and Driskoll, Kellach did not blush. Instead, he stared steadily at the dragon, as if challenging him.

"You still haven't told us why you've lied to us all this time."

"Lied?" the dragon said. "I never lied."

"You never told us who you were," Kellach pointed out.

"Would you have believed me if I had?" Gryphyll asked.

Kellach thought for a moment, then slowly shook his head. "No, probably not. But I still don't understand. Where have you been, while the evil forces have been gathering outside Curston?"

"Why, I've been searching for my medallion, of course. If you'll recall what you know about silver dragons, it will begin to make sense."

Driskoll tried to remember the information they'd studied with Zendric before they'd embarked on their quest. It seemed ages ago.

"I've got it!" he said suddenly. "Silver dragons sometimes live among humans, and when they do, they often take the form of a troll-like creature that lives underground."

"Very good, Driskoll. So true!"

Driskoll turned to Kellach. "I read about it in Zendric's book, that monster guide."

"Living below the prison, in the form that you first met me, allowed me to search for my medallion before it fell into the wrong hands," Gryphyll explained.

"But it did," Kellach reminded him.

"Yes, I know," Gryphyll said slowly. "Such a surprise. I feared the worst when Lexos found it. I was actually thinking how to get it back, when the three of you stumbled across my path. A treasure, truly a treasure."

"And that's when you decided to trick us," Kellach said.

"Kell, what's with you?" Moyra said. "Why are you being so mean?"

"Mean?" Kellach turned to her. "I think pretending to be something you're not, getting us into all kinds of trouble, nearly getting us killed—that's what I'd call mean." He turned back to Gryphyll. "Wouldn't you agree?"

Gryphyll smiled broadly. "You didn't enjoy your adventure, Kellach?"

"That has nothing to do with it. You could have revealed yourself to us, taken back your medallion, and been off. In fact, here." Kellach thrust his hand under his robes and pulled forth the pouch. Untying it, he withdrew the silver medallion from inside.

"Here," he repeated, holding the medallion to Gryphyll. "Take it."

"Kellach, if I had revealed myself to you, then there would have been no quest."

Kellach lowered his hand slowly.

Gryphyll continued. "Don't you believe that people must earn the honors they receive?"

"Of course," said Kellach.

"I didn't mean to trick you. I meant to get to know you. The quest for the silver dragon is real. I am real. And now I know that the three of you are real, too."

"Real?" Kellach repeated.

"The three of you are carrying on the legacy of the silver dragon," Gryphyll said. "As one of the last silver dragons in the realm, I wanted to be sure that the order would be in the best and most capable hands."

Kellach lowered his head.

"Please take the medallion," he said.

Gryphyll lifted it gently from Kellach's palm and closed his long fingers around it.

"You are worthy, as the galeb duhr said," Gryphyll said. "And I am proud to pass along our legacy to you."

"Oh, Gryphyll!" Moyra cried. She lunged at the dragon and wrapped her arms around as much of him as she could. Driskoll joined her on the other side, and soon Kellach joined in the group hug.

"My, my, my," an evil voice taunted from the passageway. "Isn't this touching?"

The hairs on Driskoll's neck stood up. Peering around Gryphyll's silver scales, he couldn't believe who he saw.

CHAPTER

25

L exos!" Driskoll whispered.

The old town magistrate stepped deeper into the room. His dark robes swirled around his feet, and a leather sash slashed across his chest, angling from one shoulder to the opposite hip. His long, graying-blond hair framed his old pruny face, and his knobby hands rested on a gnarled walking stick. He smiled, but the smile didn't reach his hard, dark eyes.

"What?" said Lexos. "No warm greeting for your old friend?"

"You're no friend of ours, you creep!" Driskoll said.

Lexos chuckled. "I see your journey has still left you with some spirit." He shook his head. "Too bad it has to end here."

"What are you talking about?" Kellach said. "We made a deal. We gave you the medallion."

Lexos's eyes flashed. "Do you think I wouldn't be able to spot a fake, boy? I must admit, I was fooled for several days. That bit about Zendric putting a spell on it." Lexos spat. "Nothing can replace the real medallion, not even an old wizard's handsome work. It may have taken me some time, but when I realized I'd been fooled, I knew I had to find you."

"How did you find us?" Moyra asked.

Lexos's eyebrows drew down across his forehead. "Do you think you're the only ones who know the legends of the silver dragons? When I couldn't find you in Curston, I assumed you had probably made the foolhardy quest to find the silver dragon on your own."

"But how did you catch up to us so fast?" Driskoll asked.

Lexos shot Driskoll an impatient look. "Your misadventures with the galeb duhr and the salamander slowed you down considerably; whereas, a powerful cleric such as myself can dispense with such nuisances in an instant. And once I spotted you riding the wind steeds, you weren't hard to track at all." Lexos paused and drew himself up. "Now it's time. Time to make you all pay for deceiving me, for escaping from my hut, for stealing what is rightfully mine!" His voice thundered and echoed throughout the cavern.

Gryphyll shook back his head and started to laugh, a deep, warm sound. He waved a wing, as if Lexos was no more than a speck of dust. "Oh, Lexos. You are a treasure!"

Lexos narrowed his eyes.

"A treasure, I tell you!" Gryphyll continued. "So dramatic and gloomy. It's wonderful! So entertaining."

Lexos jerked his head, as if he'd been slapped. He lifted his walking stick and pointed it at Gryphyll. "You, dragon, don't know who you are speaking to."

Gryphyll lowered his head, his long neck snaking down toward Lexos. He put his nose right up to Lexos and sniffed loudly. Lexos backed up a few steps, but no more. Then Gryphyll pulled back his head and sneezed. Dragon snot sprayed all over Lexos.

Driskoll, Moyra, and Kellach held their hands in front of their faces, trying hard not to laugh.

"Oh! So sorry," Gryphyll said. "So sorry, indeed. I must be allergic to something on your person."

"You'll pay for that, dragon," Lexos said. He used the sleeve of his robe to wipe the dragon spittle off his face. "You'll all pay!"

"Nonsense!" said Gryphyll. "You are far outnumbered."

"I have abilities, more powerful than you could possibly imagine."

"Hogwash!" Gryphyll said.

Lexos frowned. He tilted his head and studied the dragon more closely. Then he smiled, an oily, greasy, evil smile.

"Look, friend," he said, lowering his walking stick. "All I want is the medallion that was stolen from me."

"Stolen?" Gryphyll said. He scratched his chin thoughtfully with a thin talon. "Hmm. Can something be stolen if it never belonged to you in the first place?"

"That medallion is mine, dragon!" Lexos said, thumping his walking stick on the floor. "I found it buried in the floor of that cursed prison cell."

"Yes, and I suppose I should thank you for that."

"You can thank me by handing it over," Lexos said. He began to stroll around the cavern as if he owned it.

"Lexos," Gryphyll said patiently. "I know you are not stupid. Far from it, in fact."

"I'm glad you realize that," Lexos rasped.

"Then you must realize that the medallion belongs to me. If you know the legends of the silver dragons, then you must also know that a silver dragon created the medallion."

"Of course," Lexos said. "But what does that matter to me? You lost it. I found it. Therefore it is mine." He lowered his head, and peered out from beneath his white eyebrows. "You want to know what I know of silver dragons? Your kind are the weakest of all dragons. They were nearly all killed off when the seal was sundered. What's more, silver dragons are cowards. They avoid inflicting harm on others."

Lexos reached over his shoulder, then raised his arm. In his hand he now held a long, gleaming sword. "I, however, take pleasure in inflicting harm. I think I will enjoy killing you."

"No!" Driskoll shouted.

He rushed from under Gryphyll's wing and ran toward Lexos, pulling his sword from its sheath. He stopped about three feet from the old elf and tightened his grip on the hilt of his sword.

"I won't let you harm him!" Driskoll said.

Lexos raised a brow and smiled slightly.

"What's this?" he said. "You think you can beat me in a sword fight, little boy?"

Driskoll lifted his chin. "Of course!"

"Driskoll, no!" Moyra shouted.

Driskoll didn't turn around. He stared at Lexos and held his sword with both hands in front of him.

Lexos nodded. "So be it." Then Lexos raised his sword over his head and brought it down on Driskoll.

"Driskoll!" Moyra screamed. She tried to run toward him, but Gryphyll held both her and Kellach against his side.

Driskoll blocked Lexos's sword with his own, then he flung his sword upward, pushing Lexos and his sword away from him.

"I've had some training," Driskoll said. He planted his feet and lowered his sword, never taking his eyes off the old cleric.

Lexos laughed. "You are no match for me. Why don't you give up now, before you get truly hurt."

"And why don't you stop stalling and fight me?"

Lexos's face turned red. He let out an angry bellow, then waved his sword above his head, twirling it. Driskoll did the same, and their swords clashed in the air. Lexos moved his sword from side to side, but Driskoll was just as quick, and he matched Lexos, stroke for stroke.

Their swords met overhead and held. Lexos leaned in and put his face right in front of Driskoll's. "You can't beat me," he said. "I have far too much experience."

"That may be," Driskoll said, his heart pounding, sweat dripping down the side of his face, "but I'm younger and quicker than you!"

Driskoll moved his sword with lightning speed, trying to stab and jab and chop the old cleric down. But no matter where Driskoll thrust his sword, Lexos was there to meet it. Driskoll's arms began to shake and his legs began to wobble.

He's playing with me, Driskoll thought. Like a cat with a mouse.

He looked at Lexos's face and saw him smile.

With a burst of energy, Driskoll threw himself at Lexos, and they fell to the floor. The sword fell from Lexos's hand and skittered under a stone bench.

Driskoll rolled off the cleric, his chest heaving, his hair plastered to his forehead with sweat. Lexos lay on his back, then struggled to sit up.

"I can see I underestimated you." Slowly he began to stand.

"I told you I've been practicing." Driskoll raised his sword level with his stomach, prepared to fight Lexos again.

"Yes, well, you also underestimated me. Only a child would be fool enough to carry merely one weapon." Lexos's arms disappeared inside the sleeves of his robes. They emerged quickly, each holding a long, lethal dagger. "In some ways, these daggers are much more efficient than a cumbersome sword, don't you think?"

Lexos snapped his head in Gryphyll's direction and flung a dagger at the dragon.

"No!" Moyra cried. She pulled herself from Gryphyll's side and dived in front of his silver belly, her back to Lexos.

The dagger struck, embedding itself in Moyra's pack.

Moyra turned, her eyes angry and hot. Her face flushed nearly as red as her hair. She reached behind her and plucked the dagger from her pack.

"Now it's me and you, Lexos," she said.

Gryphyll put a claw on her shoulder, his talons brushing against her chest. "No, Moyra, this is not your battle to fight."

Moyra looked up at him. "I won't let him hurt you!"

"He won't. I assure you."

"Moyra, look out!"

Driskoll's shout came just in time. Moyra turned as the second dagger, thrown by Lexos, was about to stab her right through the heart.

167

Instead, Driskoll and Moyra watched, mystified, as the dagger floated harmlessly in the air.

Kellach stepped forward, his arm stretched out in front of him, his palm held up and out. He moved his arm, and the dagger moved with it. Then he dropped his arm, and the dagger dropped helplessly to the ground.

Kellach strode over and picked it up. He gripped it in one hand and set his other hand on his hip. His blond hair flowed royally around his shoulders, and his eyes sparkled.

"Do you have any more weapons, Lexos?" said Kellach.

Lexos growled. He flung his arms up, and chalices and stones and goblets began to fly around the room. Lexos waved his arms crazily, and the objects flew toward Gryphyll, Kellach, and Moyra.

Driskoll covered his head and ran toward them. When he reached them, he turned, held up his sword, and started swatting at the objects being thrown at them by Lexos's magic. Kellach stood to his right, and once again he had his arm up, palm out, trying to control the flying objects and send them back to Lexos. Moyra stood to his left, also battling the objects. From somewhere she'd found a silver serving platter, and she used it now as a shield, gripping it with both hands and smashing Lexos's projectiles.

But Lexos was determined. As soon as they sent an object back to him, he volleyed it back. Driskoll couldn't imagine how it would ever end.

Then, out of the corner of his eye, Driskoll saw a flash of silver zip across the room. It wasn't one of the objects that Lexos had hurled at them. It was—

"Locky!" Driskoll cried. "Kellach, Locky's out of your pack!"

Kellach smiled knowingly, but he didn't say a word. He stood, with his palms raised, and his eyes closed, deep in concentration.

The little mechanical dragon soared over Lexos's head, whirring and chirping angrily. He hovered in front of the cleric's face and breathed a cloud of smoke directly up his nose.

Lexos coughed and waved his hands frantically in front of his face. "Bugger off, you stupid gizmo!"

But Locky wasn't deterred. He flew forward, beating the old cleric with his wings and slashing at him with his razor-sharp talons.

Lexos was forced to raise his arms over his head to protect his face. He backed into the corner as the little silver dragon continued his assault.

"I think Locky's distracting him!" Driskoll hollered.

"And it looks like it's working!" Moyra called back.

Fewer and fewer stones, goblets, chalices, and other heavy gold objects flew through the room. Lexos's arms flailed helplessly above his head.

Locky buzzed backward, and looking over one shoulder, he chirped triumphantly at Kellach.

Kellach smiled. "I guess silver dragons aren't so weak after all, eh, Lexos?"

Then, in that horrifying instant, Driskoll realized Locky had stopped his assault a moment too soon. Ever so quietly, Lexos flicked his wrist, sending a silver goblet careening directly at the little dragonet.

"Locky, watch out!" Driskoll shouted

Locky zipped to one side, catching the goblet with one claw. He zoomed back toward Lexos.

And with one swift movement, he conked the cleric on the head with the heavy cup.

Suddenly, all the objects in the room fell to the ground. Lexos swayed and stumbled.

Locky landed on top of Lexos's head.

The cleric crumpled to the floor.

Kellach lowered his arm, Driskoll lowered his sword, and Moyra lowered her platter. They stood there for a moment in stunned silence.

Then Locky chirped.

Cautiously, the trio walked over to the pile of stones and goblets that they'd been flinging around the room. They could see Lexos's hair, but not his face, for the old cleric was lying on his stomach. His arms spread out above his head, and his gnarled fingers clenched into fists. Stones, goblets, and chalices lay scattered across and around him. He was silent, not moving.

Locky flew up and landed on Kellach's shoulder.

A weird feeling settled in Driskoll's stomach. "It could be a trick."

"There's only one way to find out," Moyra said. She nudged Lexos's leg with her foot.

"What are you doing?" Driskoll said. "Don't touch him!"

"I'm just making sure." She looked at them and smiled. "Besides, when can you kick around a town magistrate?"

Slowly, Kellach and Driskoll smiled back at her.

They heard clapping and turned around.

"Well done, well done!" Gryphyll beamed.

Moyra bowed, then ran across the room and stopped before the dragon. "We couldn't let anything happen to you."

Kellach and Driskoll followed her, a bit more slowly.

"Gryphyll," Driskoll said, putting his sword back in its scabbard. "Is Lexos dead?"

Gryphyll raised his head and sniffed the air. "Hmm. I don't think he's dead, but we won't have to worry about him any longer."

"Why's that?" asked Kellach.

"Because, my friends, we'll leave him here in the mountain."

"Can you do that?" Moyra said.

"It's my home," said Gryphyll. "I can do whatever I please with it."

"But where will you live if—"

Gryphyll shook his head, cutting off Moyra's questions. "So good of you to worry, so good! A treasure, really! But don't worry about it. We silver dragons are quite resourceful. Yes, resourceful, we are!"

Then he turned to all of them. "Kellach, Moyra, Driskoll, come. Climb onto my back. It is time you returned home."

They did as Gryphyll asked, scurrying onto his scaly back. They tried to get comfortable and find places to grab on to.

"Hold on!" Gryphyll said. He unfurled his wings, bent his knees, then with a sudden burst upward, he rammed his silver head through the rocky roof of the cavern and emerged into the meadow and the snowy world beyond.

Rock and snow and earth rained down around them, but only for a moment. Driskoll looked back, and he poked Moyra, then Kellach in the shoulder. He pointed down, to the meadow below.

They watched the meadow collapse, as if folding in on itself. The flowers disappeared, color after color after color, sliding into a hole in the ground, as if being pulled from the inside. Brown, pebbly earth took their place, like a blanket that had been pulled from a bed, revealing the straw mattress underneath. Then snow from the neighboring mountains shook loose. It rolled and surged down the mountainsides and spread across the brown earth. Snow soon covered the entire spot, until no one would ever have suspected that the meadow had ever existed.

Driskoll turned back to his friends. "I hope that holds him."

"Don't be silly," Moyra grinned. "Of course it will."

"But he's strong," Driskoll said. "I mean, he could wake up and dig his way out."

"He's not that strong," Kellach said. "After all, we defeated him, didn't we?"

Driskoll smiled. "We did, didn't we?"

Kellach slapped Driskoll's back and laughed, and Driskoll joined him. He looked back at the meadow once, but Gryphyll flew over a mountain, and it was soon out of sight.

CHAPTER

26

Driskoll peered between Gryphyll's wings and neck and saw the spire of St. Cuthbert's in the distance.

"We're almost home," he said to Kellach and Moyra. "Look."

Fields unfolded below them, their rows of crops forming a patterned quilt. Driskoll could see farmers and cows and horses in the fields, and he wondered if they could see them, flying high above. Then Curston's stone wall appeared, edging the fields, wrapping around the buildings and streets and towers that made up Curston. Driskoll could see Zendric's tower, spearing the sky, along with the obelisk in the town square.

"Do you think Dad realized that we'd left?" Driskoll asked Kellach.

Kellach shrugged. "Let's hope not."

Gryphyll flew in circles outside the city wall, descending, until finally he landed on a grassy knoll.

Driskoll, Kellach, and Moyra slid off his back and landed in the grass. They laughed and rolled, then eventually stood up and brushed themselves off. When they raised their heads, the dragon was gone, and a strange little gnome stood in its place.

"Gryphyll!" Moyra cried. She ran to his side, went down on her knees, and hugged him. His face crinkled, and he hugged her back. "A treasure, a treasure!"

Kellach and Driskoll walked over and looked down at the little man, smiling.

"I don't know which way I like you better," Kellach said. "As a dragon or as, well, as a gryphyll."

Gryphyll's purple eyes twinkled. "So true, so true! But this way attracts a lot less attention, don't you think?"

"Wait!" said Driskoll. "Where's the medallion?"

Gryphyll giggled, then pulled the chain out from under his shirt, the medallion dangling at the end. "It feels so good, so good, to have the medallion back."

Driskoll turned his eyes from the medallion. "Well, don't show it to anyone! We don't want to have to go through all that again, do we?"

Driskoll looked again, and the medallion was once more hidden beneath Gryphyll's clothing.

"Good!" said Kellach. "Now, let's see Zendric and tell him all about the quest."

"And about Gryphyll," Moyra said. "Don't forget Gryphyll." She put his arm around him and began to walk down the knoll.

"A treasure, a treasure!" Gryphyll said, waddling along beside her.

Driskoll inhaled deeply and began walking with his friends toward the walls of Curston.

The brave warrior slashed with his sword, bringing the salamander to its knees. With one exact strike, he chopped off first one icy talon, then the other. Slice, slice, slice! The icicles fell to the ground. Next he—

"Driskoll!" Kellach shouted. Sitting at the long table in Zendric's tower, Kellach was trying to read from several large books, each loaded with enchanting spells. "I'm trying to memorize these."

"Sorry, Kell," Driskoll said, resheathing his sword. "I know we've only been back a week, but I'm bored already."

"Well, be bored somewhere else!"

Driskoll walked across the room, pulled out a chair, and took a seat across from Kellach.

He drummed his fingers on the tabletop. "Can you believe Dad never suspected that we'd left Curston?" he said.

Kellach looked up. "Actually, no, I can't. All he did was ask if we'd had a nice time at Zendric's."

Driskoll snorted. "A nice time! What do you think he'd do if he knew?"

Kellach raised a hand. "I don't even want to think about it."

A knock sounded at Zendric's door. Driskoll pushed back his chair and rushed to answer it. Flinging it open, he saw Moyra, her arm around Gryphyll's shoulder. Gryphyll's amethyst eyes winked up at him.

"Hey! Come on in! Join the party!" Driskoll said.

"What party?" Moyra asked.

"Oh, you know, swordplay, memorizing magical chants, that sort of stuff."

"Sounds like fun." Moyra rolled her eyes.

"And what brings you two here this time?" Zendric asked, entering the room from a door near the back of the tower. "May I bring you a cup of tea?"

"No, sir, I'm afraid I must be off," Gryphyll said.

"Off?" Moyra drew back and looked at Gryphyll. "What do you mean, off?"

"It is time I leave Curston, my friends," he said.

"You can't!" Moyra said. "I mean, I thought you liked staying with me and my family. My mom loves all the help you've given her with her herbs and her knitting."

Gryphyll looked at her kindly. "It's been lovely staying there, truly, but now that the medallion has been found, I must return to the mountains."

"But it's so far!" Moyra said.

"Yes, but I must see if perhaps other silver dragons have survived, just as I did." He smiled. "After all, if you can restore the Knights of the Silver Dragon, perhaps the silver dragons can restore themselves."

He turned to Zendric. "Thank you, Zendric, for bringing back the Knights. And for choosing such able members of the new order."

Zendric bowed. "I'm glad you're happy with them and that they successfully completed the quest. And I'm also glad that you've forgiven me for not recognizing who you were when I first met you."

Gryphyll waved a hand in the air. "No bother, no bother, dear wizard. I didn't want anyone to know who I was until absolutely necessary."

Gryphyll turned and walked to Driskoll. Taking Driskoll's hand, he placed a small dagger on his palm, the handle studded with purple amethysts.

"Every warrior must have a dagger," Gryphyll said. "Use it wisely. Make the silver dragons proud."

"I will," Driskoll said. A lump forming in his throat, and he wrapped his fingers around the dagger's handle.

Next, Gryphyll stepped in front of Kellach. "For you, my young wizard, I would like you to have this brooch. Someday soon, you will wear the cloak of a wizard, and you will need the brooch to secure the top."

Kellach lowered his head, deeply moved. He gazed at the amethyst jewel, surrounded by braided silver. "I should not have questioned you on the mountain," he said.

"Ah, Kellach! It is always wise to question what you don't understand. That is what separates the great men, like Zendric, from foolish men, like Lexos."

Finally Gryphyll stood before Moyra. Tears brimmed her eyes, and she tried to brush them away. "I'll miss you," she whispered.

Gryphyll held out his arms, and Moyra bent down and hugged him fiercely.

"A treasure, a treasure!" he said into her hair.

Moyra straightened, but she couldn't help a few tears from splashing onto her cheeks.

Gryphyll reached up a stubby finger and wiped them away. "Moyra, you have been the best of friends." He pulled the dragon medallion from a pocket and unhooked it from its silver chain. He handed the chain to her. "I would be honored if you would wear the chain to remember our friendship."

"I don't need anything to help me remember you," she said. But she bent down, and Gryphyll placed the chain around her neck. Before rising, Moyra threw her arms around Gryphyll again and hugged him one more time.

Then she released him and stepped back.

"Come, my friend," Zendric said. "It is time."

Zendric led them to the staircase that spiraled up to the top of the tower. Gryphyll waddled and chirped bits of nonsense as they walked up the stairs, and Driskoll smiled slightly. They reached the top and walked outside onto the roof of the tower. Gryphyll hobbled to the low stone wall, while Driskoll, Kellach, Moyra, and Zendric remained by the doorway.

As they watched, Gryphyll grew taller and wider, and wings blossomed from his shoulders. Silver scales replaced his clothing, and claws replaced his hands and feet. His face changed shape, too, molding and forming until the head of a dragon appeared. Only his eyes remained the same, purple and twinkling and laughing.

"Don't forget," he intoned deeply in his dragon's voice. "The silver dragons still live."

With a quick wink and a flick of his wings, Gryphyll rose into the sky. One last time, they heard him say, "A treasure, a treasure!"

Then he disappeared before anyone in Curston was aware that a silver dragon had just graced their skies.

MORE ADVENTURES FOR THE

KNIGHTS OF THE SILVER DRAGON

™

FIGURE IN THE FROST

A cold snap hits Curston and a mysterious stranger holds the key to the town's survival. But first he wants something…from Moyra. Will Moyra sacrifice her secret to save the town?

DAGGER OF DOOM

When Kellach discovers a dagger of doom with his own name burned in the blade, it seems certain someone wants him dead. But who?

THE HIDDEN DRAGON

The Knights must find the silver dragon who gave their order its name. Can they make it to the dragon's lair alive?

Ask for KNIGHTS OF THE SILVER DRAGON books at your favorite bookstore!

For ages eight to twelve

For more information visit www.mirrorstonebooks.com

Explore the mysteries of Curston with Kellach, Driskoll and Moyra

The Silver Spell

Kellach and Driskoll's mother, missing for five years, miraculously comes home. Is it a dream come true? Or is it a nightmare?

Key to the Griffon's Lair

Will the Knights unlock the hidden crypt before Curston crumbles?

Curse of the Lost Grove

The Knights spend a night at the Lost Grove Inn. Can they discover the truth behind the inn's curse before it discovers them?

Ask for Knights of the Silver Dragon books at your favorite bookstore!

For ages eight to twelve

For more information visit www.mirrorstonebooks.com

THE NEW ADVENTURES

THE DRAGON QUARTET

The companions continue their quest to save Nearra.

DRAGON SWORD
Ree Soesbee

It's a race against time as the companions seek to prevent
Asvoria from reclaiming her most treacherous weapon.

DRAGON DAY
Stan Brown

As Dragon Day draws near, Catriona and Sindri stand as
enemies, on opposing sides of a feud between the most
powerful wizards and clerics in Solamnia.

DRAGON KNIGHT
Dan Willis

With old friends and new allies by his side, Davyn must
enlist the help of the dreaded Dragon Knight.

DRAGON SPELL
Jeff Sampson

The companions reunite in their final battle with
Asvoria to reclaim Nearra's soul.

**Ask for Dragonlance: the New Adventures
books at your favorite bookstore!**
For ages ten and up.
For more information visit www.mirrorstonebooks.com

WANT TO KNOW HOW IT ALL BEGAN?

WANT TO KNOW MORE ABOUT
THE **DRAGONLANCE** WORLD?

FIND OUT IN THIS NEW BOXED SET OF
THE FIRST **DRAGONLANCE** TITLES!

A RUMOR OF DRAGONS
Volume 1

NIGHT OF THE DRAGONS
Volume 2

THE NIGHTMARE LANDS
Volume 3

TO THE GATES OF PALANTHAS
Volume 4

HOPE'S FLAME
Volume 5

A DAWN OF DRAGONS
Volume 6

Gift Set Available
By Margaret Weis & Tracy Hickman
For ages 10 and up

KNIGHTS of the SILVER DRAGON™

A young thief.

A wizard's apprentice.

A twelve-year-old boy.

Meet the Knights of
the Silver Dragon!

SECRET OF THE SPIRITKEEPER
Matt Forbeck

Can Moyra, Kellach, and Driskoll unlock the secret of the
spiritkeeper in time to rescue their beloved wizard friend?

RIDDLE IN STONE
Ree Soesbee

Will the Knights unravel the statue's riddle
before more people turn to stone?

SIGN OF THE SHAPESHIFTER
Dale Donovan and Linda Johns

Can Kellach and Driskoll find the shapeshifter
before he ruins their father?

EYE OF FORTUNE
Denise R. Graham

Does the fortuneteller's prophecy spell doom
for the Knights? Or unheard-of treasure?

For ages 8 to 12

THE NEW ADVENTURES

JOIN A GROUP OF FRIENDS AS THEY UNLOCK MYSTERIES OF THE DRAGONLANCE WORLD!

TEMPLE OF THE DRAGONSLAYER
Tim Waggoner

Nearra has lost all memory of who she is. With newfound friends, she ventures to an ancient temple where she may uncover her past. Visions of magic haunt her thoughts. And someone is watching.

THE DYING KINGDOM
Stephen D. Sullivan

In a near-forgotten kingdom, an ancient evil lurks. As Nearra's dark visions grow stronger, her friends must fight for their lives.

THE DRAGON WELL
Dan Willis

Battling a group of bandits, the heroes unleash the mystic power of a dragon well. And none of them will ever be the same.

RETURN OF THE SORCERESS
Tim Waggoner

When Nearra and her friends confront the wizard who stole her memory, their faith in each other is put to the ultimate test.

For ages 10 and up